Swift Lightning

Swift Lightning and Mistik drew nearer and
nearer the ring of great beasts.

SWIFT LIGHTNING

A Story of Wildlife
Adventure in the Frozen North

BY

JAMES OLIVER CURWOOD

Fredonia Books
Amsterdam, The Netherlands

Swift Lightning:

A Story of Wildlife Adventure in the Frozen North

by
James Oliver Curwood

ISBN: 1-4101-0724-8

Reprinted from the 1919 edition

Fredonia Books
Amsterdam, The Netherlands
http://www.fredoniabooks.com

In order to make original editions of historical works available to scholars at an economical price, this facsimile of the original edition of 1919 is reproduced from the best available copy and has been digitally enhanced to improve legibility, but the text remains unaltered to retain historical authenticity.

SWIFT LIGHTNING

SWIFT LIGHTNING

CHAPTER I

STRANGE and mysterious whispers of the arctic night were in the air. It was twilight—early twilight—of the long gray months of sunless days that were descending swiftly upon the frozen-in world that caps the North American continent above the arctic circle. Underfoot there was less than half a dozen inches of snow, hard and fine, each particle like a granule of sugar, and under it the ground was frozen solid. It was forty degrees below zero.

Upon the bald crest of an ice hummock that overlooked the white sweep of Bathurst Inlet, Swift Lightning squatted on his haunches and gazed forth upon his world. It was his third winter—his third Long Night. And the twilight of its coming stirred him with a strange uneasiness. This twilight was unlike that of the south—it was a vast, gray, chaotic emptiness in which vision traveled far but saw nothing. Earth and sky and sea and plain mingled into one. There were no clouds, no sky, no horizon, no moon, no sun, no stars. It was worse than night.

A little later there would be many of these things, and Swift Lightning's shadow would run with him.

Now his world was a pit. And that pit was filled with sound which he had never liked, and which at times filled him with a great yearning and a strange loneliness. There was no wind, but in the gray chaos that hung under the sky there traveled moanings and whisperings at which the little white foxes yapped incessantly. Swift Lightning hated these foxes. Above all other things he hated them. He wanted to tear them into pieces. He wanted to still their voice; he wanted to rid the earth of them. But they were elusive and hard to catch. Experience had taught him that. On his crag of ice he drew his lips back until his fangs were bared. A snarl gathered in his throat, and he stood to his feet.

He was a splendid beast. Not half a dozen wolves between Keewatin and the Great Bear could come shoulder to shoulder with him in size. He did not stand altogether like a wolf. He was square-chested, and his great head held itself high. About him was little of the sneaking and cautious alertness of his brethren. He looked forth openly and unafraid. His back was straight, his hips free of the "wolf droop," and all over he was the soft gray of the brush-rabbit. His head had a massiveness about it that was strange to the wolf breed; his eyes were wider apart, his jowl heavier, and his tail did not drag. For Swift

Lightning was a throwback—a throwback of twenty wolf generations. That many years ago his forefather had been a dog. And the dog was a Great Dane. For twenty years his blood had run with the wolves, for twenty years it had bred with them, until at the end of the fifth breeding season the strain of the Great Dane was submerged in the wild-wolf breed. And for fifteen years thereafter his ancestors had been wolves—hungry, meat-questing wolves of the great barrens, wolves with drooping backs and haunches, wolves with dragging tails and narrow eyes—wolves, who did not hate the little white foxes as he hated them, and as the Great Dane of twenty years ago had hated them.

But Swift Lightning, standing on his crag of ice, a throwback of twenty wolf generations, knew as little of the drop of dog in him as he did of the mysterious wailings and moanings high up in the gloom between him and the sky. He was wolf. As he stood there, the snarl in his throat, his long fangs bared to the yapping of the foxes, he was all wolf. But in his wild and savage soul—a soul hardened to battle, starvation, cold, and death—the voice of that Great Dane forefather of nearly a quarter of a century gone was trying to make itself heard.

And Swift Lightning, as he had answered the call before, answered it now. Blindly and without reason, without understanding and with a helpless instinct within him groping for the light, he went down to the level of the sea.

The "sea" was Bathurst Inlet. As Coronation Gulf is a part of the Arctic Ocean, so Bathurst Inlet is a part of Coronation Gulf. Wide at the mouth but tapering down to the slimness of a woman's finger, it reaches two hundred miles into Mackenzie Land, so that on its ice one may travel from the grassless and shrubless regions of the walrus and the white bear to the junipers, birches and cedars below the great barrens. It is the long and open trail that reaches from Prince Albert Land down into open timber—a whim and a freak of the arctic, a road that points the way straight as a die from the Eskimo igloos of Melville Sound to the beginning of civilization at Old Fort Reliance, five hundred miles to the south.

It was southward that Swift Lightning turned his head and muzzled the air. He forgot the little white foxes. He set off at a trot and at the end of an eighth-mile he was running. Swifter and swifter raced his great gray body. In his second year a Cree and a white man had seen him running across the neck of an open plain, and the Cree had said, "Weya mekow susku-wao—He is swift as the lightning." Swift Lightning ran like that now. It was not work. It was his play—his joy in living. There was no prey ahead of him. He was not hungry. And yet a wild thrill possessed him, the thrill of quick movement, of splendid muscles, of a magnificent and tireless body that responded to his humor and his desires as a faultless mechanism responds to the electrical touch of a man's hands. In his savage way he was conscious of this power within himself. Best of all, he loved to run under the moon and the stars, racing with his shadow, the one thing in all the Northland he could not beat in a straightaway across the open. Tonight, or today—for it was neither one nor the other now—the madness of speed was in his blood. For twenty minutes he ran his race with nothing—and then he stopped. His sides rose and fell in rapid breathing, but he was not winded. His head was erect the instant his movement ceased; his eyes peered restlessly into the chaotic emptiness ahead of him, and he tested the air.

In that air was something which drew him at right angles to his tail and sent him into the thin scrub timber along the shore. This "timber" was a thing that revealed the mighty forces of the arctic. It was a gnarled and twisted Tom Thumb of a forest into which he moved—a forest warped and contorted until it seemed to have been frozen lifeless while writhing in a tempest of agony. Living for ages, it had never grown above the protecting depth of the snow. It might have been a hundred, five hundred, or a thousand years old, and its mightiest tree, as large around as a man's leg, rose no higher than Swift Lightning's shoulder. In places it was dense. And at times it was shelter. Big snow-hares popped in and out. A huge white owl floated over it. Twice Swift Lightning bared his fangs as he caught ghostly flashes of the little foxes.

But he made no sound. A bigger thing than his hatred of the white foxes was gripping at him now, and he moved on. The scent in the air grew stronger. He faced it squarely, and did not slink or cringe as he advanced. Half a mile farther on he came to a seam in the earth scratched there by a rough edge on some prehistoric glacier. It was narrow and deep and strange, more like a crevasse than a valley. In a dozen long leaps he could have spanned it. In it was timber —real timber—for each winter the winds from the barrens swept it full of snow and its trees were protected to a height of thirty or forty feet. They lay dense and black below him. And Swift Lightning knew there was life there—if he cared to seek it.

Passing along the crest of this glacier-cut crevasse, he was no more than a gray shadow that was a part of the gloom. But there were many eyes in this pit, that were born to darkness, and they watched him savagely. Out of it rose great white ghosts of snow-owls. Their huge wings purred over him and he heard the vicious snap of their murderous beaks. He saw them, but he did not stop, and neither was he afraid. A fox would have scurried for safety. Another wolf would have swung barrenward, snarling. But Swift Lightning troubled himself to do neither of these things. He was not afraid of owls. He was not afraid even of Wapusk, the great white bear. He knew that he could not kill him, but that Wapusk could crush him with one sweep of his huge paw. Still, he was not afraid. In all his world only one thing held him in awe, and suddenly that rose up before him, a shadow in the dusk.

It was a cabin—a cabin built of saplings dragged from the darkness of the glacier-slash. Out of it rose a chimney, and from the chimney came smoke. It was the smoke Swift Lightning had smelled a mile away. For several minutes he stood without moving. Then he circled slowly until he came on that side of the cabin where there was a window.

Three times in twice as many months he had done this same thing, and had squatted on his haunches and looked at the window. Twice he had come at night and each time the window had been aglow with light. It was aglow now. To Swift Lightning it was like a square patch of ruddy sun. From it poured a pale-yellow *something* out into the night. He knew fire, but until he found the cabin he had never known fire like this—a fire without flame. It was as if the world had grown dark because of that cabin, for within it the sun had hidden itself.

In his deep chest his heart beat fast, and his eyes

glowed strangely as he faced the lighted window a hundred feet away. Back over twenty generations of wolves the drop of dog in him sped like a homing pigeon—back to the days of the Great Dane, who had slept in the circle of a white man's fire and had felt the touch of a white man's hand; back to sun and life and warmth and the love of a master's voice. It was the ghost of his forefather that sat at Swift Lightning's side as he looked at the yellow window. It was the spirit of Skagen that was in him. And it was the ghost of Skagen that had run with him through the twilight to seek the smell of the white man's smoke.

These things Swift Lightning did not know. He faced silently the cabin and the light, and into his savage heart came a great yearning and a great loneliness. But not understanding. For he was wolf. Through the bodies and the hearts and the blood of twenty generations of wolves he had come. Yet did the ghost of the Great Dane persist at his side as he watched.

In the cabin at the edge of the glacier-slash, with his back to a stove, Corporal Pelletier of the Royal Northwest Mounted Police was reading aloud to Constable Sandy O'Connor an appendage to his official report, which was starting by Eskimo sledge within a few days for Fort Churchill, seven hundred miles to the south. Pelletier's last word was addressed to

Superintendent Starnes, commanding "M" Division at Churchill, and it read:

I beg to append the following regarding the caribou and the wolves to emphasize my report on the famine conditions that are bound to grip the Northland this winter. The wolves are gathering in monster packs, numbering from fifty to three hundred. On one trail we counted the bones of two hundred caribou slain within a distance of seven miles. On another we counted more than a hundred in nine miles. It is common to find where thirty or forty have been killed in smaller pack-hunts. I am told by the older Eskimos that once in a generation the wolves go "blood-mad," gather in huge packs and drive all game from the country, slaughtering what does not escape. In these years, the Eskimos believe their "devils" have triumphed over the good spirits of the land; and because of this superstition it is difficult to secure their cooperation in great wolf-hunts which we might otherwise organize. I have hope that the younger Eskimos may be convinced, and Constable O'Connor and I are working to that end. I have the honor to be, sir,

I have the honor to be, sir,

> Your obedient servant,
> FRANÇOIS PELLETIER,
> Corporal of Patrol.

Between Pelletier and O'Connor was a table of split saplings, and over them hung the tin oil lamps that lighted the window. For seven months they had stood their post at the top of the earth, and for them the razor was forgotten, and civilization a thing far off. On the map of the world there was one other place where the law was personified farther north and that was over at Herschel Island. But the barracks at Herschel Island, with their comforts and their occasional luxuries, were not like this shack. And as they sat in the glow of the lamp, the two men were a part of the savagery which they policed. O'Connor, red-headed and red-bearded, with a giant's shoulders, doubled his huge fists in the middle of the table and grinned across at Pelletier, whose beard and hair were as black as O'Connor's were red. And Pelletier grinned back, a bit apologetically. Seven months of hell and the anticipation of five more ahead of them had not spoiled their feeling of comradeship.

"It's fine," said O'Connor, admiration in his blue eyes. "If I could write like that I'd be south and not here—for Kathleen would have married me long ago. But you've forgotten something, Pelly. You didn't put in what I told you about the leaders—the leaders of the packs."

Pelletier shook his head.

"It doesn't sound good," he said. "It doesn't sound —reasonable."

O'Connor rose to his feet and stretched himself.

"Then damn the reason of it," he protested. "I say, is there reason in anything up here, Pelly? I tell you these Eskimos with their guinea-hen clack are *right*. If the devil himself ain't leading the packs, I'm black and not white and my name ain't O'Connor. I'd tell that to the Super till I was black in the face, I would. Now if we could get the leaders——"

He stopped suddenly and faced the window. And Pelletier, stiffening where he sat, also listened.

Again is was Skagen—the spirit of Skagen, and not Swift Lightning—who howled at the white man's cabin. Through his great jaws the cry came, a far-reaching lament that pointed straight up into the gray mash of the sky—a call back through those twenty generations to masters who long ago had forgotten or were dead. No wolf among the great packs had a voice that rose from deeper in the chest or reached farther into the distance than Swift Lightning's. It began low, mourning, filled with a weird sadness, but steadily increasing in volume. It was a message of life, and yet of death—a thing that traveled far in wind and storm and darkness—the one thing of all others feared, inspiring, and terrible. And the world shuddered and shrank from the sovereignty of that cry.

Thus Swift Lightning howled at the edge of the glacier-slash. And before the echoes of his howl had died away over the wide barrens the door of the cabin opened, and in its path of light stood a man. It was O'Connor. Into the grayness he stared, and his arms moved quickly, bringing something to his shoulder. Twice before this hour Swift Lightning had seen the flash of fire and heard the crash of strange thunder that followed movements like O'Connor's. The second time a thing like burning iron had seared a long furrow in his shoulder. Instinct told him it was death that hummed close over his head now—a death with which he could not cope, a death which he could not fight and himself destroy, a thing treacherous and unfair. And treacherous things he hated. For his forefather had been fair to man and beast until his great heart died. With Swift Lightning it was a heritage.

He turned, and the farther gloom swallowed him up. But he did not run. He was not frightened. Another thing than the fear of death struggled in the wild, blood-yearning soul of him now. It was the spirit of the Great Dane, fighting for survival, overwhelmed at last.

And, when again Swift Lightning reached out and sped like a shadow through the gloom, the ghost of Skagen no longer ran at his side.

CHAPTER II

THE shot—that deadly humming in the air—and again the fierce red blood of the wolf sped like a running fire through Swift Lightning's veins. Once more he was the raw, magnificent pirate of the barrens, a buccaneer of the great snows, *"kakea iskootao"*— "a hell-driver among beasts." Quickly O'Connor had wrought the change—O'Connor and his rifle.

A new pulse stirred him. The loneliness that had drawn him to the cabin and the call of a breed long dead were replaced by another and more thrilling desire—the desire to rejoin his pack. The spell was broken. Again he was wolf—all wolf.

Straight as a compass might have pointed he streaked across the barren—five miles, six, seven, almost ten. Then he stopped, and with his sharp ears thrown to the wind ahead he listened.

Three times in the next three miles he stopped to listen. The third time he heard faintly and far away the voice of Baloo giving the hunt cry to the pack— Baloo the Slaughterer, Baloo the Long-Winded, to whom size and fleetness and giant strength had given the leadership of packs. Swift Lightning sat back on his haunches and answered. From south, east, west, and north came echoes of the pack-cry of which Baloo was the center. His note was longer, more frequent, more significant; and those of the wolves who were hungry for new blood and fresh meat turned in its direction. In ones and twos and threes they trotted over the frozen ground. For seven days and nights, as hours were counted, there had been no big kill, and long fang and bloodshot eye were eager for the sight and the taste of game.

That same desire surged through Swift Lightning as it surged in the wildest of the wolves. Many of the pack had gathered and were on the move when he joined them. They ran silently, a close-shouldered, ghostly incarnation of savagery, a mighty force of jaw and fang and muscle bent on death. Perhaps there were fifty, and the number steadily increased—up to sixty, eighty, a hundred. At their head ran Baloo. In all the pack only one other wolf could compare with him in size and strength, and that was Swift Lightning. For that reason Baloo hated him. Tsar and overlord of all the others, he sensed in his rival a menace to his sovereignty. Yet they never had fought. This, again, was because of the Great Dane. For Swift Lightning, unlike any wolf that ever was born, coveted no power of leadership. In his youth and his strength, his individual prowess and his power to kill, lived the joy and the thrill and the fulfilment of his life. For days and weeks at a time he hunted alone, and held himself aloof from the pack. In those days and weeks his voice gave no response to its call. He adventured alone. He ran alone. Always alone—except that at these times the ghost of Skagen ran at his side. When he returned Baloo looked at him with red and bloodshot eyes, and the fangs of his great jaws were bared in jealous hate.

Swift Lightning, in the mastering youth of his three years, had no desire to fight his kind. He fought, but it was not the fighting of oppression, nor was it his choice; and he did not kill the conquered, as Baloo would have killed them. Many a swift gash of resentment he had taken from smaller and weaker wolves without demanding the vengeance which lay within the power of his jaws. Yet, at times, red murder ran in his heart.

It was there now. Never had the desire to kill been stronger in him, and he gave little thought to Baloo as he ran close to the head of the pack.

As the arctic fight for existence weighs heavily in the lives of men, so it is with the wolves. Baloo and his pack did not run as the forest wolves run. Their excitement was repressed, and once it had set foot to the trail the pack gave forth no cry. It was a weird and ghostly monster of a thing sweeping through the gloom like a Brobdingnagian *loup-garou* moved by the pulse of a single heart. Its silence was the silence that comes with the Long Night. One standing a distance away would have heard its passing—the purring beat of a multitude of feet, its panting breath, the clicking of jaws, a low and terrible whining.

To Swift Lightning this was his game, this his reward for living. He paid no attention to Muhekun, the young she-wolf who ran at his side. She was a slim, beautiful little beast, and all the effort of her agile young body was exerted to keep shoulder to shoulder with him. Three times he heard her panting breath close to his neck, and once he turned slightly so that his muzzle touched her back. With the birthright of young motherhood before her there had risen in her an instinct even greater than the instinct to kill. But in Swift Lightning there was no responsive thrill. The day and the hour had not come. Only one passion possessed him now—the passion to overtake what was ahead of him, to tear and to rend, to bury his fangs in living flesh and hot blood.

He was the first of all the pack to catch what a hundred muzzles were seeking in the air—the scent of the caribou herd. Another quarter-mile and it was coming up strong in the wind, and Baloo turned southwest with his horde. The speed of the pack increased, and slowly, very slowly, the monster shadow made up of a hundred racing bodies began to disintegrate, and the wolves to scatter. There had been no signal. The leader had made no sound. Yet it was as if a command had leaped from brain to brain, and each had responded to it. Daylight would have revealed a mighty spectacle and the impending tragedy. The hunters were spreading themselves over a front of an eighth of a mile. The strongest and fleetest made up the two ends of the advancing fighting-line. Less than a mile away were the caribou.

The thick gray gloom covered the onsweep of the deadly line, and the wind was against the herd of cloven hoof and horn. There was no warning and no sound.

Swift Lightning leaped suddenly ahead. For the first time he exerted his great speed. Pack-instinct, the law of leadership, the presence of the young she-wolf, who had fought hard to keep her pace beside him, were no longer a part of his existence. He sprang shoulder to shoulder with Baloo. He passed him. His speed was the speed of the wind itself. In half a mile he gained an eighth—and he was alone. The smell of living flesh was hot in his nostrils. Gray shapes loomed up in the night ahead of him, and straight as an arrow he launched himself to the kill. In that same instant came the savage outcry of the pack. Silent until the moment of attack, its throat burst now, and like an army of pitiless Huns the wolves swept down upon the caribou.

The herd was scattered. They had been digging the crisply frozen green moss from under the snow, and Swift Lightning's attack was their first warning. From

him alone they would have fled instantly and without
confusion, but terror seized upon them with the coming of the pack, and on the frozen plains there was
suddenly the beat of hoofs that sounded like the rumble
of distant thunder. The instinct of the sheep is to herd
close in time of danger, and so it is with the caribou.

Swift Lightning's rush carried him twenty yards
inside the lines of the herd, and his fangs were at the
throat of a young bull when the terrified animals began crowding upon him. In a close and crushing
mass they hemmed him in. With his hundred and
forty pounds of muscle and bone he hung to the young
bull's jugular. He heard the crash of bodies, the
snarling tumult of the pack, but no sound came from
between his own locked jaws. His brethren were at
work, two and three and four to a caribou, but it was
Swift Lightning's humor to make his kill alone. The
great herd began to move, and in the heart of the inun-
dation he and his victim went down. Not for an instant did he loosen his grip at the bull's throat. A mass
of bodies swept over them; they felt the beat of hoofs,
and about them was a rattle and crash of horns. Still
deeper sank Swift Lightning's fangs. Then for a
moment he ceased to breathe; every vital force within
him rose to the supreme effort; and with his forefeet
braced he gathered his body like a powerful spring and
flung himself backward, and the young bull's blood
gushed in a crimson stream on the hoof-beaten snow.

Twenty caribou were down when Swift Lightning staggered up from his kill. The tail of the herd had passed. The main herd, a thousand strong, was stampeding wildly to the south and west. Again it was like slow-moving thunder. No hunger could rise above the lust of the pack for slaughter, and from their victims the blood-crazed outlaws of the barrens raced after others. Exhaustion alone stopped the killings. Until their jaws were tired, and they could run no farther, the wolves hung to the tail of the herd. When the last of them turned back, sixty caribou lay dead over a blood-stained trail three miles in length.

Then the feast began on the carcasses of the animals last killed. Swift Lightning had not made his second kill alone. It had been a long fight and a hard one. His body was kicked and horned and trampled, and it would have gone still harder with him had not another pair of jaws joined his own. In the throes of that battle he had caught the inleap of a slim body; he had heard a fierce and vengeful snarling and the slash of other teeth—and when the work of death was done he found that it was the young she-wolf who had come to help him. Her jaws were red, she was bleeding from wounds and panting like a beaten and wind-run thing—yet she came to stand in triumph and joy at his side.

They had killed! That was her attitude. *They* had killed—Swift Lightning and she! And on that red field of death a thing came to Swift Lightning which he had not known when she had run at his side an hour before. It was then the instinct of her sex told Muhekun that at last she had won.

With new inspiration Swift Lightning tore a great hole in the caribou's side, and when it was large enough Muhekun joined him. Then, side by side, they began the feast. The young wolf's body lay close and warm against Swift Lightning, and he was filled with the satisfaction of the possessor and the master. He did not eat ravenously, but tore chunks of flesh loose that Muhekun might get at them more easily. And as other wolves passed them, or their snarling sounded near, her eyes roved jealously. It was she who saw the big form come up on the other side of their caribou, and pause there, looking down on her with gleaming eyes. Swift Lightning, with his mouth full of meat, heard the warning snarl in her throat but paid no attention to it. He was not quarrelsome and a dozen wolves might have fed on his caribou without disturbing his temper. But the thrill of matehood and of allegiance to her mate ran through Muhekun's blood like fire. It was Baloo who was intruding. He began tearing at the caribou, and the next instant Muhekun was at him—a vengeful flash. Her ivory fangs slashed his shoulder, and the big leader whirled upon her.

Then Swift Lightning saw what was happening and a leap carried him to Baloo. The leader's jaws were

at Muhekun's throat when he struck, and there was
a rending of flesh as the two great beasts rolled in
the snow. Swift Lightning was up an instant quicker
than his enemy. On her belly Muhekun was dragging
herself toward him. Blood streamed from her torn
throat and a strange sobbing was in her breath. Swift
Lightning heard her choking whimper, and there rose
up in him—stronger and mightier than it had ever
come to him before—the spirit of the Great Dane. Out
of the mists of the past the heart of a dog cried out,
not alone for vengeance but for justice, for the defense
of the weak, for the brute chivalry of the dog—alien
to the wolf—which demands the protection and cham-
pionship of the female. To Baloo, the gashing of
a she-wolf's throat meant no more than the slashing of
a male's. To Swift Lightning, for the first time in
his life, came a blind and terrific desire to avenge.

Baloo was up and facing him, even as the dying
whimper in Muhekun's throat ended in a choking gasp.
Slowly, hardly more than an inch at a time, they began
to circle, and, as they circled, wolves that were near
left their feasting and gathered about them in a red-
eyed and watchful ring—the death ring out of which
only one of the fighters would come alive. Baloo, the
true wolf, circled with a cautious, slinking movement.
His ears were alert, but his body sagged like a gathered
spring, and his bushy tail dragged on the snow. Swift
Lightning, with all the appearance of the wolf, stood

differently. From head to tail he was erect and tense,
every muscle in him ready for the life-and-death struggle. He was only half as old as Baloo, which was to
his advantage in the matter of strength and endur-
ance. But Baloo all his life had been a fighter. He
was cunning, a trickster, sharp as a fox in his strategy.
Suddenly he swung inward, and so unexpected and
lightning-like was his movement that, before Swift
Lightning could either evade or meet him, the other's
fangs had laid open a six-inch gash in his rump.

Clever as the old warrior's attack had been, his get-
away was still cleverer. Scarcely had he struck his
blow when Swift Lightning lunged at him with all his
gigantic strength, and Baloo—instead of leaping to
right or left—did the unexpected thing, and flattened
himself so adroitly that Swift Lightning passed half
over him. Baloo flung his head sideways and upward,
and his teeth slit like knives in the other's belly. It was
a deep cut, and Swift Lightning's blood flowed freely.

Both strikes had covered a space of not more than
twenty seconds, and in an ordinary wolf-battle an im-
mense advantage would have rested with Baloo; for a
twice-stricken wolf whose own attack has met with defeat, is no longer a game fighter, but accepts the great
handicap and greater hazard of defensive instead of
offensive action. Here was where Swift Lightning's
heritage from old Skagen put a checkmate to Baloo's
triumph and strategy. A second time he leaped at his

enemy, and a third time he was slashed—this time in the shoulder. For an instant he was down, but only for an instant. A third time he rushed Baloo, and for the first time jaw clashed against jaw. A roar filled his throat. His fangs closed with a terrific crunch, and Baloo went down and under, twisting and snarling. For a quarter of a minute their jaws were locked. Then Baloo twisted himself free, and again with that deadly sideways fling of his head he knifed Swift Lightning deep in the chest.

Swift Lightning's blood already reddened the wolf-ringed arena, and the scent of it filled the air. Baloo was bleeding from his jaws. Thirty or forty of the pack had gathered in an ominous circle about the fighters, and the others were joining it. Muhekun had not moved since her last effort to drag herself to Swift Lightning. A pool of blood had gathered under her throat, and her eyes were growing dim. But she faced the fighters, keeping them within her vision as long as she could see.

Swift Lightning saw his elusive enemy now through the flame of a blind and terrific rage. He did not feel his wounds. It was the soul of Skagen that fought in his great body now. He no longer pranced and circled in the wolfish way. His huge shoulders hunched aggressively; he lowered his head; his pointed ears lay flat and there was no sound in his throat as he drove at the leader of the pack. Again and again Baloo cut and slashed, and through those slashings Swift Lightning rushed for the death-hold. Twice he almost had it. The third time he got his hold—at the back of his enemy's neck. It was an all-dog hold. He did not rip. His jaws simply closed—as Skagen's jaws would have closed—and, even as the circle of red-eyed wolves edged nearer, Baloo's neck snapped and the fight was over.

It was a full minute before Swift Lightning loosened his grip and staggered away, and in that instant the waiting hordes piled upon Baloo, tearing his dead body into ribbons. It was the law of the pack, the wolf's age-old instinct to outrage the fallen.

Swift Lightning stood alone at the little she-wolf's side. Muhekun tried to raise her head, but failed. Her dying eyes closed. Twice she opened them, and with a whine Swift Lightning touched her muzzle with his own. She tried to answer, but all that came was a strange sob in her breath. And then, suddenly, a tremor ran through her beautiful young body, a last sigh, and she no longer struggled to breathe or open her eyes.

Over her Swift Lightning stood, and he knew that death had come. He waited a moment, and then sat back on his bleeding haunches and pointed his head to the sky. And the wolves that were tearing at Baloo heard and understood, for out of Swift Lightning's throat came the cry of mastery, of triumph, of leader-

ship of the pack—and in that cry was also a note of
grief and of sorrow. The soul of Skagen, after twenty
years, had come to overlord the wolves.

A few days later, in the cabin on the edge of the
glacier-slash, Corporal Pelletier added another and final
postscript to his official communication to the superintendent of "M" Division, at Fort Churchill:

> Since writing the above, the wolves have made
> another big kill, and the caribou are drifting still
> farther south and west. With Constable O'Con-
> nor I shall organize at once a great hunt of the
> Eskimos along this part of the coast in an effort
> to exterminate at least a part of the monster pack
> that is driving all game from the eastern barrens.
>
> Respectfully,
> FRANÇOIS PELLETIER.

CHAPTER III

THE sombrous darkness of twilight was gone and the arctic world lay mellow and golden in the lap of the Long Night. High up where the midday sun would have been in a southern summer sky hung a steady, silvery illumination, the faintly gleaming mother-of-pearl heart of the night itself; and close about this silvery heart were the stars. Countless and still, fixed and lifeless things blazing everlastingly in the sky, they lightened the frozen world like unmoving and jealous eyes watching enviously the scintillating and more spectacular glory of the aurora.

Tonight, or today—for night and day exist in terms of hours even where there is neither day nor sun—the aurora was like a many-robed magician. For two hours *Kesik Munitoowi*—the sky-goddess—had been at play, and as if to disprove her kinship to the pole she was displaying her mysterious charms and phosphorescent splendor over what would have been the western horizon. For two hours she had been unfurling her banners of all the colors of the rainbow; for two hours she had frolicked in her dazzlement of flame and glow. She had sent out ten thousand dancers of sinuous and twisting beauty; she had

streaked the sky with pathways of gold and crimson
and orange and diamond-blue, and now—as if tiring of
her more intricate sport—she was beginning to paint
her playground a vivid, living red. In city, village,
and open land a thousand miles to the south were eyes
that saw her and wondered at the mystery of the thing
"over the pole." But it was *under* her that souls shivered, and the ice of a frozen world flung back a glow
to the stars.

This world was dead, white, and still. It was ter-
ribly cold, so cold that in the air—unmoved by a breath
of wind—were at times steely crackling sounds. Now
and then, from out of the mountainous ranges of ice
in Coronation Gulf, came an explosion that was like
the rumble of a great gun as one of the ice mountains
broke or split to its heart; and when these explosions
came their echoes ran like whimpering, ghostly things
up the frozen surface of Bathurst Inlet, for the play
of that intense cold was as weird and mysterious as
the aurora herself. At times it was as if a company
of skaters were flying through the air on ringing
steel, and one could fancy the swish of their skirts,
the sound of their voices and far-away laughter. Yet
one would not have sensed the deadliness of the cold,
for without wind it held no bitterness or sting.

Outside their little cabin of saplings stood Corporal
Pelletier and Constable O'Connor, and not far behind
them was a hooded and furred Eskimo with a sledge

and six-dog team. It was a month and a half ago that Pelletier had sent his last report down to Fort Churchill, and, as he looked at the vivid crimson splash of the aurora in the west, he said:

"The first red night of the winter, O'Connor. It's lucky for us. It means plenty of blood to the Eskimos, and I'll wager every conjuror between here and Franklin Bay is busy at work this minute casting out evil spirits and offering up prayers. The hunters along the coast ought to be on their way to join us to a man."

O'Connor shrugged his shoulders with the skepticism of the unbeliever. He had great faith in Pelletier and he loved with a man's love this picturesque and storm-hardened Frenchman who had lived half of his life along the edge of the arctic circle. But he had his own opinion of the gigantic wolf-hunt he had faithfully helped Pelletier to plan. For two weeks his clumsy fingers had rolled strychnin poison in pellets of caribou fat. He had faith in the poison. Scattered over the wide barrens, those baits would bring death to something. But as for the hunt——

"It's our one chance—and theirs," Pelletier was saying, still looking at the red sky. "If we can get the big pack into a cul-de-sac, if we can destroy even a half of it, we save five thousand caribou. And if Olee John doesn't fail us with his reindeer we'll do it. If we succeed, it means we'll be staging big hunts

up and down the coast all winter, and if we don't get
a sergeancy and a corporalship out of it——" He
grinned hopefully at O'Connor.

"We'll at least have the fun," finished the Irishman.
"Let's move, Pelly. I'm guessing the thermometer
is close around forty right now. Ho, you—Um Gluck;
get a move on! Mush it! We're on our way."

The Eskimo in his furs came to life. His voice rose
in a clacking chatter; his long whip curled over the
backs of the dogs, and eager for the thrill of the
trail they leaped out in a straight, tawny line, whimpering and whining and clicking their jaws in their
yearning for the long run under the growing crimson
of the sky.

For many miles up and down the savage coast of
Coronation Gulf and the rugged shores of Bathurst
Inlet there was movement that night. The scourging
hand of famine lay threatening over the land, and this
movement was Pelletier's awakening of the igloo people, their response to the "call" of the White King,
who was to turn a great magic against the devils that
possessed the devastating hordes of wolves that were
driving all game from the barrens.

The tribal camp of Topek was to be the rendezvous.
It was Topek's runners who carried word of the great
wolf-hunt up and down the coasts, and it was Topek
who sent the warning that, unless the wolves were

driven off or destroyed, famine and death would fall heavily upon the land. Faithfully he repeated the message of the police, represented by Corporal Pelletier and Constable O'Connor.

There was a thrilling answer to the summons. For unnumbered generations the benighted people of Coronation Gulf had lived in the belief that devils entered into the bodies of the blood-mad wolves in wintertime; and those who answered the call of Topek and the police were the youngest and bravest of them all. It was one thing to give battle to the big white bears, but quite another matter to turn human hands against the evil spirits. Yet they came, and two hundred hunters headed for Topek's village. They were protected by many charms and armed with many weapons. A few had rifles, purchased in times of plenty from the whalers; some had harpoons, and others assagai-like lances with which they hunted the seal. From farthest west of all came Olee John, an Eskimo who had married a woman in the white man's way, and with him came ten of the bravest hunters of his village, and a herd of fifty reindeer.

The aurora, like a lamp burned out, had faded away when Pelletier and O'Connor came to the end of their six-hour journey and shook hands with Topek and almost hugged Olee John. For six hours thereafter the hunters continued to come in. With the last of them a terrific wind filled with sleety, shot-like snow drove from over the ice fields. It filled every track and wiped out all trails. And for three days and three nights after that storm, by the hours of Pelletier's watch, there was great activity in Topek's camp. The cul-de-sac was found—a "blind cañon" with ice walls and only one entrance—and the work of luring the wolves into it began. Five times the reindeer herd went forth, guided by Topek and Olee John and Olee John's men; and five times it came back, men and beasts near exhaustion. Yet no cry of wolf came from the reindeer's trail, and no great pack followed it. And although hundreds of poison baits were scattered in the hoof-prints of the herd no dead wolves were found.

In the stolid faces of the young Eskimo hunters began to grow a solemn fear. The medicine-men and the elders of the tribes were right—devils were in the wolves, and they might as well fight the winds. Even Topek and Olee John were losing faith, and in Pelletier's heart was an ever-growing anxiety.

For the sixth and last time Topek and Olee John and the reindeer herd went forth upon their errand, and there were those in the village who whispered that outraged gods and devils were about to set their curse upon the land and sea.

CHAPTER IV

SWIFT LIGHTNING and his great pack of wolves were heading north. Thin-ribbed and gaunt and with backs and haunches drooping from days and nights of futile questing for meat, they were scattered like a beaten army in retreat. Since the night they had slaughtered the greater part of the caribou herd, they had made only one big kill. Then had come a week of storm, and after the storm the caribou were gone. There was no longer scent of hoof on the barrens. In a world trackless and illimitable they had disappeared as utterly as though they had never been. But forty miles to the west, hugging the hollows of the coast plateaus for shelter, Swift Lightning could have found them, and the pack would now have been fattening at the tails of the thinned and scattered herds.

Had the eyes of Topek's people seen the return of the pack into its old hunting-grounds, every god of the Eskimos would have been called upon for protection. For it was no longer a superstition that devils traveled in the bodies of the wolves. They *were* devils, and the hunger-madness was in their hearts. In other beasts starvation works its natural way—the animals crawl off and die; in the wolf it is a poisonous toxin. Under

a billion stars and the silvery illumination in the sky,
Swift Lightning's pack, a hundred and fifty strong,
traveled in deadly suspicion of itself. In truth they
were pirates now—pirates watching for the opportuni-
ties to slit one another's throats. Red-eyed and sleep-
less, their jaws white with the frozen drool of hunger,
they watched and listened for the snarl and clash of
fang that meant one more victim among their comrades. There was no howl or outcry as they crossed
the barren. A moving, spectral horde of gaunt and
thin-ribbed shadows, they made their way silently
through the night.

Swift Lightning alone had escaped the madness. He,
too, was starving. His giant body had grown thin.
His eyes were red. A flaming desire possessed him,
but his heritage from Skagen—that one drop of dog—
had saved him. The dog abhorrence of cannibalism
was strong within him. A score of times he had seen
the pack rush in to fight and rend in its monstrous
feast over a carcass of its kind. But he had held himself aloof, in his throat now and then—instead of the
snarl of murder and hate—was a faint and yearning
whine, and as the pack neared its old hunting-ground
he felt once more the lure of the white men's cabin on
the edge of the glacier-slash. He had not forgotten
the purring, deadly thing that had passed over his
head—the bullet from O'Connor's gun. But desire
rose above fear. Again it was Skagen, the dog of

twenty years ago, who answered to the glow of yellow sun within the cabin, the smell of smoke, and to that *something* which Swift Lightning, the wolf, could not understand.

He drifted back into the heart of the pack until the shadowy forms were traveling all about him. Among them he was a giant. He heard the snap of jaws in the gloom when he shouldered too near another of his clan. But he did not slink or cringe as he ran. He sensed the deadliness of those snarls, yet he felt no animus in return; and as he drifted he made his way to the east. In that direction the cabin lay. It was not logic that drew him. The cabin had given him nothing but the smell of smoke and the yellow glow, and out of it death had sung close over his head. Yet he went, his body moving mechanically to the impulse that lived in his brain. At the edge of the pack he stopped and watched the last of the starving shadows as they passed him. Then he headed north and east.

His speed increased. It was not the speed of the Swift Lightning who, a few weeks ago, had run like the wind down the frozen surface of Bathurst Inlet. In his movement was no longer the pure joy of running. His muscles had ceased to respond like living wires to the thrill of action. His feet were sore. A steady and aching distress lay between his ribs. The snap was gone from his jaws, the keenness of swift vision from his eyes, and his breath came short and quick in less than half a mile. When he slowed down he was panting. For a space he stood and listened. Starving, he still held his great head erect, and in the starlight his eyes gleamed brightly as he faced the direction of the famished pack. He did not want to go back to it now, and he did not want it to follow him. In his aloneness there fell upon him a new freedom. The pack was gone; the gnashing of teeth and the snarling of throats were gone—and he was glad. The air was clean, no longer heavy with the hot scent of mad beasts. Ahead of him lay the night, open and far-reaching, and filled with new promise.

What that promise might be was a thing of no definite fact in his mind. In all his world the one thing he wanted most was something to eat. He turned in the direction of the cabin and for a quarter of an hour he kept on. He was traveling with the wind, and twice he stopped for an instant to test it out. The second time he stood longer than the first, for he caught faintly a scent in the air—the wolf scent—and he growled. Half a mile farther on he stopped again, and the growl was deeper and more menacing. The scent was stronger than before, and yet he had been moving steadily away from the pack. He increased his speed, and in him began to grow a sullen resentment. The wind was his book. It was the one thing that held all knowledge for him, and it told him that back in the night something was following him.

A fourth time he stopped. The scent was stronger.
His pursuer had not only kept pace with him but was
overtaking him. This time Swift Lightning waited,
and his hair stiffened and his muscles grew tense for
battle. It was not long before he saw a shadow advancing in stealthy, slinking silence. It stopped not
more than fifty feet away. And then, a step at a time,
it approached him, and Swift Lightning gathered himself to meet an enemy. Almost within leaping distance it stopped again, and this time Swift Lightning
saw that it was a huge gray timber-wolf who had joined
the pack far down in the scrub forest at the southern
edge of the barren. As large and as dark as Swift
Lightning was this wandering wolf of the big timber.
Bred in the southern forests, wise in the ways of white
men, trap-bitten and battle-scarred, Mistik the Wanderer had come north with the pack.

In the light of the stars the two great beasts faced
each other. In that light Swift Lightning's naked
fangs gleamed, his lips drew back, and he began slowly
the deadly circle. Mistik did not move. With steady,
questioning eyes he watched Swift Lightning. His
jaws were closed. There was no answering battle
light in his eyes. Unafraid, he stood without movement in the center of Swift Lightning's narrowing
circle, offering no challenge and betraying no enmity.
Slowly the snarl died out of Swift Lightning's throat,
and his flattened ears grew erect. And then he heard

from Mistik a low, throaty whine. It was an offer of friendship. It was as if the great wolf, missing the shelter of his timber, were trying to tell him that he was tired of the madness and starvation of the pack, that he had come to hunt with him alone, and that he did not want to fight but wanted to be friends.

Swift Lightning sniffed. Stiff-shouldered and still suspicious, he thrust in his head. Again he heard the low whine in Mistik's throat, and this time he answered it. A foot at a time, circling slowly in the maneuver, they drew nearer and at last their muzzles touched. A deep breath rose out of Swift Lightning's chest. He was relieved. He was glad. And Mistik whined again and rubbed close to his shoulder, and together they looked ahead into the night in this first hour of their comradeship.

It was Swift Lightning who led the way north and east. His head was higher and he sensed the presence of a new thing in his life—a new kind of comradeship. Mistik felt Swift Lightning's approval of him as they sped through the starlight shoulder to shoulder. The timber-wolf did not run as the pack wolves ran. Bred of the forests, he was more watchful and alert. Swift Lightning's vision was ahead while Mistik's was ahead and on both sides. At intervals it was Swift Lightning's custom to stop dead in his tracks and sniff the back trail; Mistik, with quick, sidewise swings of his head, caught the back-trail scent as he ran. To his in-

stincts the pitfalls and the trickeries of the forests were
still about him; to Swift Lightning the open barrens
held no concealment for treachery or peril. In his
knowledge of things it was the pack that was deadly.
Alone under the stars were freedom and safety.

Had Pelletier and O'Connor seen them as they ran,
something of the majesty and sovereignty of the wild
must have impressed itself upon them. And Aoo, the
conjurer at Topek's village, would have sworn by his
gods that he had seen the two greatest devils in all the
North racing on a mission of their own. For the
two great beasts ran inch to inch in height. In length
Mistik was the greater of the two, but in jaw and
chest Swift Lightning made up the handicap; so that
in a fight one would have hesitated to choose between
them. But in Mistik's head was much that Swift
Lightning had yet to learn, for Mistik had fought his
way in a white man's world. His right forefoot was
deformed from the bite of a trap, and he had almost
died from the torment and fire of a poison bait. He
had discovered the peril of deadfall and snare, and it
was the white man he feared above everything else in
the world.

So it happened that when they came within scent
of the cabin it was Mistik who drew back with a sudden warning snap of his jaws. His spine shot erect;
his ears grew flatter; and he circled widely in the wind,
his great body no longer free but sinuous and slinking

with the caution of the hunter and the hunted. Swift
Lightning faced the window. There was no light
in it tonight, and neither was there smoke in the air.
He approached nearer, and behind him he heard Mistik's ominous whine. Circling the cabin cautiously,
he came into all quarters of the wind. The scent was
cold.

After a little he knew that life and light and smoke
were gone. The cabin was dead. The thrill died
out of him, and he trotted boldly toward the window,
nearer than he had ever gone before. Then he sat
down on his haunches and looked steadily where he
had seen the glow of yellow light. A hundred yards
behind him sat Mistik, and in those few seconds of
their silence a gulf as wide as the barren itself lay between them. For in Swift Lightning there grew a
slow and compelling desire to throw back his head and
howl before the dark window of the empty cabin, just
as he had howled at it when there was light. When the
cry came, Mistik slunk farther back, for in it was a
note that troubled him, a note that he had heard far
south in the howling of the dogs. He circled until he
came to the edge of the glacier-slash, an eighth of a
mile below the cabin, and it was there Swift Lightning
joined him.

For weeks the slash had been catching the wind-
blown drift of the snow like a great furrow, and in
places it was filled almost to the brim. Where this

had happened the gnarled and twisted tops of trees lay sprawled out on the surface like the grotesque and agonized hands of monsters smothering underneath. In other places the humors of the wind had left deep dark pits where no snow had gathered at all, and into these pits Mistik's eyes blazed like coals of fire. It was there, and not in the open barren, that he saw their first promise of meat, and with the noiseless stealth of the forest wolf he slunk down into the deepest and darkest of them all. Swift Lightning followed.

He felt the shroud of tree tops growing overhead. The brilliance of the stars was shut out. He was traveling in a darkness which he did not like, and in that darkness Mistik's eyes were red and green points of flame when they turned his way. Twice he heard the snap of powerful snow-owl beaks not far away. Once Mistik made a terrific lunge at a ghostly shadow that swept so close over their heads they could hear the purr of its wings. Out of this pit they climbed over a mountainous drift into a second, and here also they found no smell of meat. Then it was that Swift Lightning took the lead. He clambered again up to the level of the barren and Mistik followed him as he set out for the Tom Thumb forest in which he had seen the big white hares weeks before.

Neither of them ran now. Their exertion in the crumbling avalanches and uncertain footing of the pits had betrayed more than ever their weakness.

Hours ago they had passed through the physical rack of hunger, and the process of starvation had developed beyond the stage of acute and muscular torment in their bodies. Its gnawing pain was gone from between their ribs. In its place was an increasing and at times almost irresistible desire to lie down. A little while ago it was the cabin that had urged Swift Lightning to greater exertion. Now it was the century-old "forest" of junipers and cedars that grew no taller than the crook of a man's arm, and his brain was filled with dancing visions of big white hares.

They came to it and passed into it. Most of it was choked and smothered under drifted snow. Here and there were places swept clean by the wind. In all his life in the thick and tangled swamps of the South Mistik had never seen anything like this grotesque and misshapen forest of the arctic world. Its trees, some of them hundreds of years old, were like sprawling octopuses. As Nature had made human dwarfs, so with her intense cold had she made deformed and club-footed hunchbacks of the junipers and cedars. But there was no meat here. Even the little white foxes that Swift Lightning hated were gone. Famine lay upon the Tom Thumb forest as heavily as it lay upon the barren.

In Swift Lightning there was still one last homing instinct—the instinct that was drawing the starving pack. On the trails of the old hunts were many bones. Now that his visions of the hares were gone, meat ceased to exist in his comprehension of things. He saw the bones. He saw them lying thick where once the snow had run red with warm blood. Toward the bones he set out, and Mistik—strong in his faith even as his strength ebbed away—kept with him neck to neck.

An hour later they came upon the broad and beaten path where for the sixth and last time Topek and Olee John and Olee John's reindeer herd had traveled over the open barren. It was warm and rich with the smell of meat. The air still breathed the fragrance of steaming flesh. Swift Lightning's heart leaped into his throat, and Mistik trembled beside him. Every desire of hunger flamed up in them anew, painful and terrible again, as desire is roused in the thirst-dying man who sees the rippling water of a mirage close ahead of him in the desert. In those moments they breathed deeply and stood still, while their bodies, like machines straining to a new task, gathered themselves for the final tremendous effort. Their blood ran swifter, their heads shot erect, the fagged muscles of their shoulders and legs hardened as they stood, and in their poise was a fresh alertness. They had not only struck the trail of a herd, but the herd was near, and instinctively they were listening to catch the beat of its hoofs.

And then Swift Lightning sat down in the middle

of the reindeer trail and with his gray muzzle pointing up to the stars he sent back over the barren the
hungering, wailing meat-cry of the pack. And Mistik,
squatting on his haunches beside him, opened his great
jaws to add voice to that cry, so that together they sent
far and wide over the windless plains the summons to
the hunt. From a mile away came an answer. From
two miles another. Voice carried to voice, until the
white world shivered to the thrilling news, and starving, thin-ribbed shadows raced in like ghosts from out
of the night—a hungry, savage horde, pitiless and
unpitied, scourging Huns of the upper lands, fiercest
of all fighters for the meat of life. And the way of
their craving stomachs led this time straight to a white
man's trap!

CHAPTER V

WHERE the early slashings of winter storm had piled the ice high on a finger of land between Arctic Sound and Bathurst Inlet was the cul-de-sac—a great fissure half a mile in length between ragged walls of ice and snow, a glacier-chasm with but one opening —a trap from which there was but one escape. At its neck it was a hundred yards in width, at its end less than twenty.

Into this trap Topek and Olee John had driven the reindeer herd. Not once but six times had they driven them between the ice walls, and for the sixth time the reindeer were in their ice stockade midway between the mouth and the end of the cul-de-sac. Pelletier's scheme was simple, and—if it worked—deadly. Vividly he had pictured the success of it in his mind. Hot on the trail of the reindeer the pack would rush in, and from their concealment close to the mouth of the crevasse a hundred hunters would drop in behind them, and at the reindeer stockade there would be many more to protect Olee John's herd from harm. The pack would be driven to the narrow end of the cul-de-sac, and there it was that Pelletier figured the great slaughter would be made.

Topek, uncovering his hooded ears to listen, was first to get the far-away shot of a gun that signaled the gathering of the wolves. An instant later came a nearer shot, and then a third, not more than a mile out on the barren; and before the echoes had died away the voices of Topek and Olee John were repeating the swift commands of Pelletier and O'Connor, Topek at the mouth of the crevasse and Olee John at the herd stockade. With the first was Pelletier, and with Olee John was O'Connor. For the space of three or four minutes there was swift movement at the opening and the middle of the trap, the subdued clack of excited Eskimo voices, the running of feet, the rattle of breaking ice, the clink of weapons as the hunters adjusted themselves in their hiding-places.

Then fell a deep and tragic silence. Pelletier shivered in the warmth of his coat even as the blood raced in hot suspense through his body. Far away, faint as a breath in the wind, he heard a wailing cry—the distant tonguing of the pack. For a passing flash his heart was struck by that sound, and he felt the prick of conscience—and regret. The Frenchman had fought all his life against the hardships of the North—"a wolf's fight," he had told himself often when a hard and perilous task lay ahead of him. And now, after all his planning, in the moment of his triumph, there fell upon him the unfairness of his trickery. It was not a fight. It was not even a play of wits. It was

a massacre of hungry things that he had staged in
the cul-de-sac—a massacre of empty stomachs, a killing
of creatures who wanted something to eat. It was
this *hungriness* of it all that pressed upon him as he
raised his hood still higher and listened to the growing
cry—for more than once had François Pelletier fought
his savage world for a taste of meat to keep the soul
alive in his body.

And he wondered, as he prepared to kill, if after all
the Eskimos and their dirty gods had a greater right
to live than the clean-born, hungry wolves.

At the head of the pack ran Swift Lightning, and at
his side was Mistik. Once again the pack was running
in hunt formation. But it was not silent, as when it
had hunted the caribou herds a month ago. Scent of
the reindeer, warm and thick in their nostrils, excited
the wolves as the taste of flesh itself. Their starving
cry reached to the stars. It went moaning and shiver-
ing for miles over the frozen barrens. In Topek's village women and children and old men heard it, and
grew silent with fear.

Three miles ahead lay the entrance to the cul-de-sac,
diminishing swiftly to two and then to one. The
voice of the pack died out, and in a hundred and fifty
throats there was a panting, grasping, swallowing of
breath, and in a hundred and fifty lean bodies the
straining of every nerve for the last great effort. The
fires in those bodies were burning out. The strongest

of the wolves forged ahead, and the weaker fell back. At the tail of the pack a line of exhausted beasts, still fighting to be in at the kill, ebbed off into the starry gloom of the barren. A dozen leaps in advance of their nearest followers Swift Lightning and Mistik led the killers. The mountain of ice loomed up ahead, and had there been a thousand men on each side of the trail the pack would not have stopped. Blind and deaf and insensible to all things but the smell of meat, the famished beasts swept on between the yawning lips of the crevasse. Straight ahead shot Swift Lightning and Mistik—on past the hundred human butchers waiting to wall them in, on past gleaming eyes that watched them from behind crags of ice and hummocks of snow, on to the corral of piled-up blocks of ice behind which the reindeer were cowering; and at their heels came an avalanche of hungry ones.

It was then that a man-made hell let itself loose in the cul-de-sac. There rose a scream—the scream of Olee John, and a shout—the shout of O'Connor; and following those cries came the shrieking yells of a hundred voices, the crash of firearms, the rattle of harpoons, the hissing of spears in the air. Above it all rose the shrieking of Olee John. For Olee John, first of all, saw that the plans of men had gone astray. Even as the rifles cracked and the horde of hunters swarmed out to give closer battle, starving beasts were hurling themselves in great leaps over the top of the

reindeer corral. As thirsty men face death for a drop
of water, so they forgot everything in the presence of
meat, and from the corral rose the thunder of hoofs,
the crashing of bodies, and the cries of horned beasts.
In the pack death ran red and fast. A score of rifles
sent into it a leaden hail. O'Connor's automatics
streamed steady trails of flame. Spears hurled through
the air with deadly precision. And yet the hungry animals continued over the top of the corral in a resistless
flood.

Within that corral ran death as red as in the beaten
snow outside. Sheeplike, Olee John's herd met its
end. Swift Lightning was already tearing at a throat,
Mistik at another. All around them was rending of
throats, scent and taste of blood, and famished jaws
filled with flesh.

In the battle-front of men, gone mad with rage
and despair, Olee John was screaming his wild lament
in Eskimo. The white men were liars! The wolves
were devils! The missionary gods were cheats and
frauds—for they were giving up his herd to slaughter
under his very eyes!

In his despair he lost fear and leaped upon crawling
and wounded beasts with a great club. A score and a
half of wolves were down, and some of them were still
living. A frothing pair of jaws snapped at O'Connor
as he dashed to the corral. Over the top he looked
in. What he saw was a twisting and writhing mass,

a terrible and formless pit of death in the starlight. Desperately he fired a fresh clipful of cartridges into the heart of it, and he yelled for the men with spears and guns. Olee John's herd was doomed; it was already down; a hundred and twenty ravenous jaws were tearing at its flesh. But O'Connor saw where the wolves might also be slain as the price of the sacrifice. He turned to yell his commands, and what he saw brought his heart into his mouth. The Eskimos had turned. They were running away! Even the bravest of them were crying out that no wolves that ever were born would kill and feast under the eyes and guns and spears of hunters a hundred strong. These were devils! These were beasts into which had entered the black souls of monsters—and they must fly before those monsters left the flesh of the herd for their own!

Vainly O'Connor called upon them. Olee John alone hesitated for a moment, then fled with the others. And fear gripped O'Connor then. Not fear of devils —but fear of the monster beasts when they had finished the herd and found him there alone!

After the rabble of Eskimos hurried Constable O'Connor, one of the two bravest men that ever set foot north of sixty-six—and Olee John, seeing him coming, shrieked louder than ever his curses against white men and white gods, and sped himself up until he was leading the flight.

Half-way up from the mouth of the cul-de-sac Topek

and Pelletier and the wall of hunters met the flight. Before it had reached them they heard the wild exhortations of the terrified hunters to fly. The night rang with voices shouting the tragedy and the devil-miracle at the corral; and the second line of hunters wavered and broke. For a space Topek tried to control them. But his voice was drowned. Pelletier's voice was drowned. And, when Olee John himself ran up, wild-eyed and shrieking blasphemy, brave Topek himself turned in the direction of his village. Then came O'Connor, running, panting, and cursing under his breath; and when there was no longer a hunter in sight the two white men followed gloomily in the trail of flight to the village to Topek.

So it happened that there was great feasting in the corral of the white man's trap that night; and, as he had questioned himself in what he had thought was the hour of his triumph, so now, in his defeat, did François Pelletier wonder at the significance of this thing that had happened—that fate and Olee John should have driven a herd of reindeer fifty miles down the coast in time to save the lives of a starving pack of wolves.

CHAPTER VI

A TERRIBLE and deadly thing is the long polar night. It is immolation of all things that make for life and light, the curse of a celestial error, the blight of a defect in the intricate mechanism of a solar system—terrible, and yet magnificent; deadly but at times rarest of all the earth's beautiful things. In the early twilight comes its warning.

As in the cabin and shack of the forests far south dark-eyed descendants of the French *voyageurs* still believe in the *feu follet* and *loup-garou,* and as they tell their children wonderful tales of the ghostly *chasse-galère*—the Flying Dutchman of the skies—and of the singing of the *"chanson du voyageur"* by those spirit-men who have neither flesh nor blood—so, in this polar night, the Eskimos tell one another that the evil spirits are at large and that the medicine of the devils has covered the face of the sun. After that the billion cold stars and the moon and the laughing aurora look down on the battle of life against death, and under skies painted and banner-strewn in marvelous colors men and beasts hunt and starve and die.

There is no end to the glory in the heavens, no end to the struggle underneath. There is no end to the freezing of the sea, no end to the eternal quest of hungry stomachs, no end to the tragedy played out in this starlighted and aurora-painted Colosseum at the end of the earth—no end, until the power of the evil spirits is gone and the earth's back twists to the sun once more. Then comes spring, summer, and plenty again for those who have fought and lived.

Yet now and then, at rare intervals, comes what is known as the "break." It is then as if the powers on high had themselves grown tired of the monotony of the struggle and were offering a diversion. The temperature rises swiftly. Compared with the former cold there is almost a warmness in the air. And with this phenomenon many things may happen.

It was the third night, as hours are counted, after the slaughter of Olee John's reindeer herd by Swift Lightning and his pack. It was a night vibrant with electrical thrill, a night trembling with magnificent witchery, a night filled with unaccountable and mysterious things. The stars were crowded in the sky and luminous as points of white fire. The moon was a living thing. Aurora stood like a giant sorceress, her head a hundred miles above the surface of the earth, shooting through the heavens electrical volleys that took the form of the opening and closing of a huge umbrella of many colors.

Under this display of radiance rode a terrific wind. The moaning and wailing of it filled the frozen world until, at times, it roared with cyclonic fury. Yet it was so high that not a breath of it touched the earth, and the miracle of it was that between the earth and the heavens there was not a cloud. To those who listened and watched from below it was the "ghost-storm," and strange thrills and weird fancies filled their souls.

This thrill and his old yearning to be alone were upon Swift Lightning. The moaning of the storm, which he could not feel, the vividness of the night, and the electrical thrill of the skies stirred like sharp wine in his veins. For a space, when these humors came upon him, he ceased to be all wolf. Then he became the throwback and the spirit of the Great Dane came to run with the wolf in his body. There swept upon him a change which thrilled him and yet which he could not understand—a yearning for something he had lost, for a thing he had never known—the call of the dog coming to him through the mystery of the years.

It was upon him now. He had come out of the cul-de-sac in which the reindeer had been killed and stood alone on the frozen, shrubless barren. It was the wind more than the vividness of the stars and moon or the play of the aurora that filled his desires with a foment of unrest and a strange excitement. He wanted to run under that wind, as the dog runs, for the sheer joy of running—and he wanted to run *alone!*

He ran straight with the wind. This was not wolf caution, but it was in Swift Lightning to run tonight

without caution, for he was neither hunting nor afraid.
The grown wolf does not play. His life is grim and
sober. But tonight, with that drop of dog riding
through the blood of twenty wolf generations, Swift
Lightning felt upon him the desire to play. And in itself that desire was a mystery to him. For, like an
adult who has never known childhood, he did not
know how to play. The soul of the dog whispered to
him in a strange language. He wanted to understand;
he wanted to answer. And the only response he could
give to that demand for play that came up to him
through the generations *was to run!* And because he
had no living comrade, he ran with the wind.

Always he ran with the wind when it moaned and
wailed between him and the stars without touching
the earth in its passing. It was his plaything. It
was a thing he could run hard, and yet could not beat.
It urged him; it taunted him; it laughed at him—and
it laughed with him. Tonight it was to Swift Lightning almost a living thing. At times it was so high
that he thought it was getting away from him entirely;
then of a sudden it would sweep down until it seemed
just over his back, a weirdly frolicsome thing urging him on to still greater madness of speed. At these
times Swift Lightning would give a sound in his
throat which the wolf and the malamute and the husky
never make. It was almost a bark—a panting, joyous
defiance to the voices in the wind.

Mile after mile he kept up the pace. His tongue hung out; his breath shortened, and at last he stopped. He sat back on his haunches and gathered his wind. More than ever a man would have called him dog now. He was laughing. With that dog laughter of his jaws and tongue there was an unwolfish and apologetic hang to his ears. The wind had beaten him again, as it had always beaten him. It had gone so far ahead of him that there was no longer sound of it, and he looked up inquiringly at the stars and at Aurora, everlastingly opening and closing her giant umbrella. For many minutes there was a strange calm in which he listened and watched. Then came the moaning of the wind again from behind him. His ears drooped lower. His jaws closed in crestfallen acknowledgment of defeat. The wind had not only beaten him—it had circled clean round him and was coming up from behind again, taunting him to another effort.

His long gray body leaped out like a flash. Only once or twice in his life had he run as he ran now. Yet the wailing and moaning voices that raced in the wind were always passing him, one after another, each calling to him as it left him behind. When Swift Lightning stopped the second time he had run five miles. This run had not tired him. His tremendous speed simply winded him. His body was still charged with the intoxication of the night. But he did not race again with the wind.

The edge of his superfluous vital energy was smoothed down, and he trotted through the vivid glow, now watching and listening expectantly for other things. What these things were he had no definite notion. They were not things he hunted, for he was not hunting, and had no desire to hunt. It is thus a dog wanders on star-bright and moonlight nights in a land where there are kennels and white men. Thus, years ago, had Swift Lightning's ancestors wandered, jog-trotting under the moon, wayfaring in the highways and the lanes and the fields, questing vagrantly and aimlessly in the sheer joy of life and its mystery. And in this fashion Swift Lightning went on, seeking the mystery ahead of him—the strange *something* that was pulling him through the night.

He had traveled for two hours when the weird and jestful wind threw something unexpected in his path. On a slope of frozen plain, under which the moss lay luxuriant, Mistapoos, a mighty arctic hare, and a score of his friends had gathered to "face the wind." In storm the big arctic hares always do this—face the wind, keep their eyes shut, smell, and listen. It is their one overwhelming instinct, keeping them from danger, just as the "Stop! Look! Listen!" signs warn travelers of the peril of passing trains. For in the tumult and blinding sweep of storm wolves and foxes and ermine slip up unexpectedly. And tonight Mistapoos and his company, wise in many things, but stupid in this, thought there was storm. There *must* be storm, they reasoned, even though they could not feel it. The sound of it was a din in their big ears. For a long time they had heard it sobbing and wailing and sweeping high up over their funny big heads—and for a long time they had sat stoically, facing the direction from which it came. They looked like big, puffed-up white cushions scattered over an area twenty or thirty feet square. Mistapoos must have weighed close to fifteen pounds, and he and his kind—in spite of any age they may carry—are the juiciest, tenderest morsels on the barrens.

Now it happened that Swift Lightning struck this bit of plain in another brief, mad spurt of running. He was not trying to beat the wind over his head, but he *was* beating the surface wind, and therefore he traveled ahead of his scent. He was coming so fast that he had no time to look for game, and Mistapoos and his company heard the sound of his feet before they smelled him. Their eyes popped open like so many lantern-shutters, and in the same moment they saw Swift Lightning upon them and he saw them. There was no time in which to choose direction, and every one of the twenty fat hares popped into the air as if released by springs. Mistapoos, whose Sunday name was *Lepus Arcticus*, made one mighty lunge. It may have been in his head to jump clean over Swift Lightning, but he was heavy and fat and full of years, and like a solid shot he landed against Swift Lightning's chest.

The impact of his fifteen pounds was so great that Swift Lightning was knocked half off his feet. Mistapoos fell with a thud, the wind and all common sense jolted out of him. Instantly his strong hind legs shot out like powerful springs, and he took another jump—again without wasting precious time to look. This time, head on, he landed in the hollow of Swift Lightning's ribs, and the mightiest of all wolves was bowled over like a tenpin hit with a ball. With a snarl Swift Lightning gathered himself up and faced the enemy. But Mistapoos, alias *Lepus Arcticus,* had disappeared in leaps twenty feet long. And gone were all of his company.

Beaten by the wind and knocked over by a rabbit, Swift Lightning lost all direct initiative for a few moments. Squatted in the center of the warm-scented space where Mistapoos and his company had "ridden out the storm", he looked askance at the world in general. And, when he rose to go, there was a slouch to his back and tail as though he feared some of his friends might have seen his ignoble defeat and would peddle the news broadcast tomorrow. In his head sizzled a new and comprehensive impression—a newborn and swiftly developed conviction that the world and things in it were not always what they seemed to be. Possibly the white things he had encountered were

not hares at all but polar bears! For surely it was not
Mistapoos, the rabbit, who had jolted the wind out
of him and knocked him down!

His good humor returned as he went on. During
the next hour the night changed again. The wind
went out of the sky. Aurora opened and closed her
umbrella for the last time and gathered her pigments
into a sea of pale-yellow glow. Where there had been
a tumult of sound there was now a vast and unbroken
silence. The surface air, hardly perceptible in its
movement, shifted until it came from out of the northwest.

Swift Lightning's run had carried him many miles
from the pack and far into the barren. Now he
changed his course to take in the faint surface wind,
and headed for the coast. He had burned out the
fire of his first riotous exhilaration, and every instinct of the wild was keen and alert in him again.
His sensitive olefactories read the night as he advanced. In his movement there was anticipation—expectation—yet, for a long time, no sign came to him.
He struck the rough, ice-smothered rim of the sea and
followed it for a mile or two. Every three or four
hundred yards he would stop and listen and sniff the
air in all directions. Suddenly he came to a cup in
the plain that sloped straight down to the shore of
the frozen ocean.

Hardly had he halted at the crest of this cup when

an instantaneous message telegraphed itself to his brain. Something was there—something in the glowing hollow which he could not see. A quiver of excitement shot through his body. He waited, fighting to translate the warning into a mental picture of what it was down there. He failed, and began to descend slowly. So cautious was his approach that it was a quarter of an hour before he reached the narrow finger of plain along the shore and saw what it was that had hidden itself in the white star-mist.

It was an Eskimo igloo. It was not the first time he had seen this type of human habitation. He had always evaded them, for the igloo was synonymous with savage beasts trained as bear dogs, and men ready to attack. It held no lure for him such as that of the white men's cabin on the edge of the distant glacier-slash. But tonight something held him. It was in the air. It was in the silence. It was in the empty desolation of the narrow strip of plain. And it pulled him nearer.

It was a small igloo, built of blocks of ice and frozen snow and pieces of ship timbers—the driftage of wreck and disaster. It looked like a big mound of snow or a huge old-fashioned beehive painted white. Its "door" was about fifteen feet long. In reality this door was a tunnel of ice and snow about three feet in diameter through which the Eskimo owners had to crawl to reach the one large room in their house. By having the opening fifteen feet away from the living apartment much cold was kept out, and the heat generated by human bodies and wicks of moss burning in seal-oil was kept in. It was a crude sort of thermos-bottle arrangement. Once the temperature was raised to fifty degrees above zero inside, and the flap to the door closed tight, the temperature would remain fifty degrees above zero for many hours—especially if there were people within to help with the warmth of their bodies.

The flap of untanned sealskin was drawn close now. Yet everything by which Swift Lightning's actions were directed told him there were neither dogs nor men in the igloo, and there was no smell of them in the air. Many footprints were in the snow but they were cold. He drew still nearer. In spite of every instinct of caution something was pulling him. Three, four, five—a dozen times he circled the igloo, and at last he stood with his nose almost touching the closed three-foot door of the tunnel. He stretched forth his neck and sniffed at the crack of it. The thick odor of man, of woman, and of beast came to him, and with that odor came a sound. It was a sound that sent him back, his head thrown up, his eyes glowing. He trotted a hundred yards in the direction the last trails had taken and then returned to the igloo. Again he smelled the odors—and again he heard the sound. He trembled. He whined. His great jaws clicked.

Through many generations of wolves a voice was

calling to him, the voice of a creature who had trusted him, and who had played with him and loved him for countless years before Christ was born—the voice of a living thing at whose feet dogs had worshiped and for whom dogs had fought through all time. In the dark igloo at the end of the tunnel a baby was crying!

It was a new thing to Swift Lightning. He had heard the whimper of wolf pups. He had heard them cry. But this was different. Every nerve in his body responded to it as a tuning-fork responds to the vibration of a piano string. It startled him, held him and filled him with a strange uneasiness. He trotted in the opposite direction and sniffed the air restlessly, striving to gather something of the mystery from his environment. A third time he went back. He smelled round the edge of the igloo and paused at the opening again. There was silence now. For a full minute he listened.

Then it came again. It was a cry that mothers would have recognized over all the world—mothers with white breasts, brown breasts, and black—the hunger-sobbing of a child. In this savage shelter on the rawest edge of the earth it was the same cry that came from the mouths of hungry babes in the palaces of millionaires two thousand miles away. It was a cry old as the ages, a cry unchanged by ten thousand years of races and creeds, a cry of the same language so far as east goes east and west goes west. To all the hearts of the world had God made intelligible that cry, and in its plaint was the thrill of motherhood, of home, of love—and Swift Lightning whimpered in reply.

Had Skagen been there—the Skagen who had known babes and children—he would have gone into the igloo; and in the darkness he would have laid his great body down beside the creature that was calling, and would have trembled in his worship and gladness, when baby hands dug their tiny fingers into his hair, and a baby voice ceased its sobbing to coo at its new-found comfort.

And the spirit of Skagen was in Swift Lightning's body as he stood at the closed door of the tunnel. It wanted to go in. After twenty years it yearned again to feel the touch of baby hands, to hear the soft cooing, to lie down once more close to the tiny, help-less creature that the great Arbiter of things had cre-ated to be its master—and its god. But that spirit was struggling for its desires in a body that had come down through generations of wolves, and the body failed to respond to the desire.

Swift Lightning felt the surge of the call—yet was he powerless to answer it. With the dog growing stronger in his soul, the blood and the instincts of the wolf were the guiding powers of his physical move-ment—and, while something went out of him and into the igloo, the blood and bone and muscle of him failed

of that miracle of understanding which alone could
have changed him into Skagen.

He circled restlessly in the bit of plain about the
igloo until he could no longer hear the crying of the
baby. Even then the impulse to continue in his wandering failed to urge him. Swiftly and strangely there
had developed in him an instinct of ownership. He
had come down into this cup of the barren, filled with
the glow of moon and stars, and found a thing in it
that was greater than the white men's cabin—a thing
that held him, that dissipated his loneliness, that stirred
him with nerve-tingling excitement. It was not a
mental picture of a baby in the igloo, for he had never
seen a baby. It was the crying, the age-old appeal of
it, the note of helplessness in it, its hunger and distress.
Swift Lightning did not incarnate the sound. It was
a mystery to him, just as the almost human voices
with which he had raced in the wind that night were
a mystery. But this strange thing in the igloo was like
an electric magnet that had dragged him for a space
out of savagery and was holding him tight.

A score of times he wandered aimlessly about the
bit of plain. It was beaten with the footprints of
man and dog, but the footprints no longer held scent.
To human eyes the story of the igloo and the plain
would have been clear. Something had happened.
For in the igloo the temperature was down to freezing.
And a baby was almost dead of starvation.

Swift Lightning sensed impending action. Just as an hour earlier he had anticipated the coming of events so now his anticipations were even more keen and eager. He was more watchful. He was constantly listening. He sniffed the air from different points and nosed the cold trails. The igloo itself was the one definite and outstanding fact in his mental comprehension. He found the nearness of it a growing satisfaction, and half a dozen times he flung himself down beside it, not to rest but to wait—and watch. It was *his* igloo; yet he sensed the insecurity of his tenure. He expected something to happen, and he was prepared to flee—or fight.

He wandered a little farther, to the edge of a huge scarp of ice that overlooked the frozen sea. Something told him it was off the sea the interruption would come, and his eyes pierced the starlight suspiciously. The wind was against him, quartering from the west. Twice he caught dimly the movement of a ghostly shadow that he would have smelled had the wind swung east. His body quivered as he tried to distinguish it a third time. It did not appear again, and he trotted back to the igloo.

Ten minutes later the shadow came up over the mountain of ice where he had stood and entered the strip of plain. It headed for the igloo. Swift Lightning saw it when it was a hundred yards away, and he sprang up, every muscle in his body tensed like

steel and ready to be unleashed. The shadow ad
vanced, growing whiter and whiter in the night-glow
until he could see the drooping, slowly swinging head
of the "gentleman in the white jacket"—Wapusk, the
polar bear.

Fifty yards away Wapusk stopped. His huge head
swung like a pendulum from side to side and his little
eyes glared. Hunting had gone unfortunately for him
and he was hungry. He was old and terrible and
merciless. A sound, so faint that it was like the far-
away rumbling of a moving ice field, rolled in his deep
chest as he saw Swift Lightning.

Sufficient unto all wolves is the roll of that thunder
in Wapusk's chest, but tonight something had risen
new-born in the soul of Swift Lightning. He did
not run from it. From his own throat came a snarl,
tigerish in its ferocity. He sensed invasion. He had
expected something, and Wapusk had come. Therefore Wapusk was the evil and the mystery which his
instincts had anticipated. His mind did not travel
beyond that fact. Wapusk was there, his huge head
swinging slowly from side to side, the murderous
rumble in his throat, his eyes gleaming. It was not
for Swift Lightning to know just how deliberately and
with what intention the big white bear had come up
off the ice; but now that Wapusk was here he knew
that his deadliest of all enemies coveted his own possession—the igloo and what it held. And he snarled

forth his defiance and his warning. His long fangs were naked as he backed himself close against the hide-covered door of the tunnel.

The big bear approached slowly. His great feet crunched in the frozen snow; his long, flesh-ripping claws rattled, his head still swung like a pendulum. It was that swing of Wapusk's head that drove fear and horror to the hearts of all living creatures. Facing it now, Swift Lightning backed still closer against the sealskin flap. A peg loosened and the flap budged inward. It was then, coming clearly through the tunnel, that he heard once more the thrilling sound from within the igloo. The baby was crying again. The sound reached Wapusk twenty paces away, and for a space the huge bear's head seemed to cease its movement. Then the rumble in his chest deepened to a roar, and he advanced like a slow-moving avalanche upon Swift Lightning.

Swift Lightning felt the giving-way of the flap, and as Wapusk made his first lunge at him he sprang back so that he stood well within the tunnel. Here he was at an advantage. Wapusk's great head and shoulders filled the passageway, leaving the mighty beast no room for action, and instantly Swift Lightning seized his opportunity. He lunged at Wapusk. His fangs tore and slashed like knives. He ripped the big bear's nose open, and Wapusk's roar of pain and fury rocked the igloo. Yet he could do nothing but advance in the face of that terrific fang-slashing. He was not a jaw-fighter alone, as Swift Lightning was; he needed his arms and his body, and these he could not use in the tight-fitting tunnel. For perhaps a minute he stood Swift Lightning's bloody punishment. Then his huge body gave a mighty heave, and that part of the tunnel in which he was wedged gave way and crumbled about him. He had shortened the entrance to the igloo by a third of its length.

Swift Lightning was almost caught in the outheaval. He leaped back still farther into the tunnel and Wapusk crowded in a second time. As Swift Lightning had fought Baloo in the madness of his first death-struggle for pack leadership so now he fought the polar bear. He tore at Wapusk's nose and face. He ripped off a half of one of the invader's ears. He caught one of the huge paws that reached out for him, and in that hold Wapusk's foot was bitten clean through. The bear's roaring could have been heard half a mile away. His body heaved again and the walls of the tunnel gave way for another five feet. He was winning although the floor of the passageway was drenched by his own blood. One more outheaving lunge of his body and he would reach the igloo itself.

With his forefeet still in the tunnel and half of his body in the igloo Swift Lightning waited for Wapusk's last triumphant attack. He felt the nearness of the end. He knew that in the mysterious open space at his back he would be no match for his mighty enemy. Yet he did not think of escape. With his head and shoulders squarely in the tunnel he not only defied Wapusk—he challenged him. And for a few moments, in the face of those savage fangs, Wapusk hesitated. His little eyes, accustomed to darkness, told him he had almost reached the inner door to the igloo. One more rush and the battle would be over, and he would be eating flesh.

In those precious moments another thing happened. Up through the plain ran swiftly three furred and hooded figures—Nepa, the Eskimo, and his wife and son. Open water had trapped them in a hunt for seals. They were returning and had heard the roaring of Wapusk at their door.

The bear did not hear them or scent them. A third time he forced his way into what remained of the tunnel. Nearness of death impresses itself poignantly upon the beast, and Swift Lightning knew that his time had come. Every nerve and sinew in his powerful body he gathered in a last mighty effort. For a space of seconds his attack was so furious that Wapusk, with lowered head, failed to heave his body against the sides of the tunnel. Perhaps half a minute was saved before Wapusk flung his weight against the walls—and the door to the igloo was open. Even as the blocks of ice and snow fell apart a human scream split the night, and a harpoon flashed.

It sunk into Wapusk's shoulder. Like very demons the hooded creatures were screaming. Swift Lightning leaped out of the avalanche in which the great bear's last attack had half buried him and came face to face with the woman—the woman for whose baby he had fought his greatest fight and had been ready to die. In her hand was a long seal spear, and with a cry of fury she flung it at him. It struck him in the flank. He felt the stinging pain of the steel, and as he fled the handle dragged for a space and then tore the barb from his flesh.

At the crest of the ridge from which he had first looked down into the strip of plain Swift Lightning stopped for a moment, bleeding and exhausted. Even then a strange whisper rose in his throat as he swallowed hard to get his wind. At last the mystery of the night had cast aside its shroud and stood naked to his understanding. And with that understanding he turned again into the frozen barrens. No more did the spirit of Skagen and the joy of the night run in his blood as he headed in the direction of his wolf pack and the slaughtered reindeer herd of Olee John. For, as he went, the wound that hurt him most was the wound made by a human hand.

CHAPTER VII

IN THE days that followed Swift Lightning's adventure at the Eskimo igloo many things happened to dim the memory of the spear thrust he had received there. Chief of these was the tightening of the grim hand of famine over the Northland. The caribou herds had drifted still farther south and west. Great storms had covered their retreat, and the wolves, whose migratory instincts were less keen, had lost the trails that would have lured them into a land of plenty far off toward the Great Bear. On the barrens they fought and starved and died; for the law of the survival of the fittest was on the land from the shores of Keewatin to Franklin Bay; and with it cannibalism walked hand in hand among all things that lived on flesh and blood. Swift Lightning himself was a hungry, thin-ribbed, savage shadow in quest of food. Since the night three weeks ago when he had led his wolves to the slaughter of Olee John's herd, hunger had pressed him hard. He traveled again in company with Mistik, and they kept the life in their bodies by digging up and eating the frozen moss from under the snow.

Swift Lightning held close to the coast and the

habitations of the Eskimos along Coronation Gulf in these days of starvation and death. His pack, a hundred and fifty strong when it had come from the far scrub timber, was disintegrated and gone. Broken by hunger and dispersed by necessity the horde no longer "rode with the devils" under the white stars, with Swift Lightning at its head. Over the barrens came no more the hunt-cry, for if a wolf killed at all he kept the meat to himself and guarded it jealously to the last bone.

For a week Swift Lightning and the big timber-wolf killed no meat, and never had they hunted as in that week. They ranged the edge of the barren, the shore, and the rim of ice fields. Half a dozen times they came upon foxes, but the little white will-o'-the-wisps of the barrens easily lost themselves in the chaos of the night. Once Swift Lightning pounced upon a seal, but it was a new quarry and slipped away from him before he could discover a fatal hold. Twice they saw big white bears, mighty beyond their power to kill. But not once in all that time did they see a hare, where there should have been thousands. Then came the last and greatest of their disappointments. In the heart of a storm they struck the trail of a musk-ox and followed it until, far out on the barren, the tracks were obliterated by the sweepings of the blizzard.

Flat on a narrow glacier-cut ledge in the face of a

mountainous upheaval of rock they were lying now, watching for a thing they had seen just ahead of them in the ghostly white gloom of the night. For a quarter of an hour they had crouched like creatures frozen stiff. Fifty feet away the rock wall swung seaward, and twice a great white shadow had floated out from it and back again. And now a third time it floated for an instant within the vision of their red eyes and disappeared.

Wapinoo, the owl, had not seen them. He, too, was starving, and the hour had come when his murderous heart was set on cannibalism. He was a monster of his kind. His wings were five feet from tip to tip. His claws were like knives and long enough to disembowel a wolf had there been sufficient flesh-ripping strength behind them. With his powerful beak he could break the skull of a fox. And he, too, was watching. But his eyes, ablaze with the madness of hunger, were not on the ledge where Swift Lightning and Mistik lay. They were gimleting straight out into the starlit gloom. What he had seen he knew he would see again. Three times it had come, and three times he had floated out, but the moment had not been right for his swooping drive. Deadly in his caution, Wapinoo waited. And a fourth time he prepared to strike.

Up the face of the rock wall, circling a little nearer each time in his silent questing for game, came a stranger owl. In Wapinoo's head was no instinct

of fear. All his life he had been powerful and no other
owl had ever beaten him in a fight. He had driven off
or killed every poacher on his hunting-grounds, and in
his strength and supremacy he was a ravager and a
bully. In a fit of rage he had slaughtered his own
family last breeding season, and starvation made him
even more terrible now. He held back, not to measure
the size and prowess of his victim, but for a better
opportunity to strike. He was blind to the fact that
Nizpak, the stranger, was as large as himself; and he
did not know that two days ago Nizpak had killed a
half-grown fox and was better fed, or that Nizpak,
in his own hunting-preserve, was an even fiercer and
more bloodthirsty pirate than he.

The fourth time that Nizpak floated in, his gleaming eyes on the alert for game, Wapinoo dived from
his hiding-place like a great white shot. He did not
strike with talons or beak, but, attacking obliquely
from above, he deliberately struck with his shoulder.
It was a mighty and well-aimed blow; Nizpak was
thrown off his balance in flight, and in the air was
much like a staggering man on his feet. A second
time Wapinoo swooped down, and with a thunder of
monster wings the two old murderers flopped to the
frozen snow of the plain. Wapinoo's advantage was
great, and his assault would have killed an ordinary
owl very shortly. One huge wing beat the dazed Nizpak like a club. With a throaty squawk of rage and

triumph he buried his talons in Nizpak's thickly feath-
ered breast, and with his powerful beak he hammered
to drive a hole in the stranger owl's skull.

But Nizpak was a buccaneer who had grown tough
in battle. With his free wing he began to beat back,
and never in all his bloody life had Wapinoo felt the
force of a wing like that of his enemy. It beat down
his own, it toppled him sidewise, it forced him to give
up his deadly hammering of Nizpak's skull. But his
talons sank deeper. Through feathers, skin, flesh and
bone they drove, and once in, the claws curved and
held, though Nizpak in another moment had swung
him over on his back. And now it was Nizpak's beak
that did the hammering. It drove like sharp iron into
Wapinoo's face. It gouged out his eyes and dug like
a chisel through the holes into the brain. Long before
it ceased the deadly work Wapinoo was dead, and
Nizpak tugged and pulled until he freed himself from
the hold of the claws in his breast.

Slowly and silently as the battle raged Swift Lightning and Mistik had drawn nearer. Slinking forward
on their bellies they were within fifty feet of the owls
when Nizpak freed himself from his dead enemy's
talons. And then, swift as shadows, their gray bodies
leaped through the night. Nizpak saw them, and with
a beat of wings, launched himself upward. But the
death-wound in his breast had weakened him, and he
rose slowly. He was six feet in the air when Swift

Lightning gave a mighty spring, and his jaws closed in a mass of feathers. A second time Nizpak crashed to earth, and with a snarl Swift Lighting's jaws flashed from feathers to the big owl's head. A crunch of bone—and Nizpak was dead.

Mistik was already tearing at old Wapinoo's tough flesh, and before Nizpak's wings had ceased to flutter Swift Lightning was at his own feast. Ravenously the two tore the feathers in great mouthfuls from the bodies of their prey, for in spite of their ferocity and strength Wapinoo and Nizpak were ninety percent feathers, and of each there were probably only three or four pounds of flesh and bone. The flesh was tough with the toughness of cartilage, whit-leather, and gristle, but to Swift Lightning and Mistik it was sweeter than caribou liver in times of plenty, and they devoured it to the last scrap.

As drink and food bring back life and hope to a starving man, so did their meal put new strength and courage into their bodies. Their reasoning, if such a process went on in their heads, was simply that famine had ended. At last they had found meat, and had eaten it. Tomorrow did not trouble them; their blood began to run warm and eager again, and their first instinct was to greater endeavor—for their appetites were only moderately appeased. Many times the big timber-wolf had tried to pull Swift Lightning southward, for in that direction Mistik knew of com-

fortable forests and game-filled swamps which he had
foolishly abandoned to join the wolf pack. So now
he set out boldly, and spurred on by the meat within
him to a new and more thrilling adventure than owl-
killing Swift Lightning made no protest.

Never had the stars burned brighter over them. The
aurora, as if shamed to modesty by their beauty, had
ceased its flamboyant play and glowed with a soft and
silvery illumination. In all that white and frozen
world there was no other thing, animate or inanimate,
as dark as the wolves' gray coats. Life itself was
white, where there was life. The big bears were white;
the owls and the hares were white; the foxes were
white; and even the color of the caribou and the
musk-ox—darker because in the time of peril nature
made them seek safety in quick herd formation—
shaded in illusively with the star-mist and ghostly
emptiness of the night. It was Mistik, accustomed to
the forests and swamps, who used his eyes and ears
most in their quest for game. But experience had
taught Swift Lightning that it was in the air he must
seek for the presence of meat. Mistik could hear a
sound a greater distance away, could perhaps see a
little farther, but long before sound or sight the wind
bore message for Swift Lightning.

As they went on, each was alert in his own way.
Every instinct within them was alive for action, and
they hunted straight south, full in the face of what

little air was stirring. The temperature had risen since the storm, and it was so still that Swift Lightning's howl would have carried over an area of twenty square miles of hunting-ground. All life, it seemed, was gone.

Yet neither of the two hunters felt the misgiving or the threat of famine. Fairly well fed once more, their hopes were built again on immediate expectation and promise. They progressed steadily but without an instant of carelessness. Once in the first half-dozen miles Swift Lightning stopped dead in his tracks and gave the low whine that told Mistik to stop, for in the wind he caught faintly the scent of a fox. He could not place its direction, and in a moment it was gone.

For another six miles they kept straight ahead to the edge of a torn and twisted upheaval of arctic bad land. Here, in ages gone, great glaciers had played with the earth. The barren was pitted and pockmarked with hollows and rock traps and back-broken ridges. It was not often that either the foxes or the wolves hunted here, but Swift Lightning and Mistik went in. To Mistik it was a land of promise. The everlasting sweep of the plain was gone, and here were hiding-places for living things. Instinct told him he was traveling in the direction of his forests, and in that direction he was determined to go.

For two or three miles their trail had led them into the broken tundra when Swift Lightning whined again. They stood on a crest of earth and rock, and a second time there had come to him a scent in the air. This time it was not the scent of fox or of hare or owl. It was big game, and a quiver of excitement ran through him as a stronger breath of wind bore it more clearly to his nostrils. Mistik caught it then. It was the pungent, woolly scent of Yapao, the musk-ox. To Mistik it was a thing alien to his forests farther south, a mystery which he sniffed at curiously and with anticipation. Swift Lightning thrilled to the marrow of his bones. It telegraphed to his brain the presence, somewhere near, of the mightiest of all game preyed upon by the wolves.

He led the way down the slope of the ridge into the hollow and sped swiftly and noiselessly ahead. Again it was intuition and unforgetable experience that made him hold neither to one side nor the other of the wind, but as directly in the face of it as he could, for Yapao was the keenest of all the barren-land creatures to smell the approach of danger. Even as Swift Lightning and Mistik slipped like two shadows between snow hummocks and masses of rock, an old bull stood rigidly in the center of a narrow strip of plain that circled, like the curve of a saucer, three hundred yards west of them. It was this "westing" of the bull that gave him his first faint scent of enemies, for in progressing full in the wind Swift Lightning and Mistik passed, by a considerable distance, the tip of the curve in which Yapao was standing. Still another three hundred yards south directly in the path pursued by the wolves, Yapao's herd was scattered in huge dark blots over a couple of acres, almost motionless as they dug up the moss from under the snow.

Yapao, of the herd of twelve, was the oldest and the largest. He was a huge and grotesquely shaped monster. He stood no higher than four feet at the shoulder yet he was eight feet long, and his head— facing at right angles the advancing danger—was like a giant, bone-plated battering-ram. Nature had intended him for the farthest north of all living creatures, for the arctic circle was the *southern* and not the northern limit of his feeding grounds. His body was round; his legs were extremely short and heavily built; his hair was thick, and so long that it trailed in the snow under his belly. Under this hair, covering the body with a protection impenetrable to cold, was a two-inch growth of wool. Even the soles of Yapao's feet were covered with hair as dense as felt, and the only bare spot on him from one end to the other was the tip of his nose. Covering the top of his great head like a steel shrapnel protector was a broad plate of bone, curving gracefully behind each eye and terminating on each side in a sharp, bayonet-like horn. This was his shield, his bulwark of defense. With it he fought defensive battles. For Yapao, seldom assaulting his enemies, was content to let them batter out their wind and possibly their lives against this fortress of his head.

For scarcely more than a few seconds did he stand silent. Then out of his throat rolled a husky bellow. It was perhaps more like the blat of a ram than a bellow, though it was hoarser and deeper-throated. In the mighty silence of the barren it was like the note of a deep drum. Instantly there was a rumble of startled hoofs, and here it was that nature made the darker color-scheme of the musk-oxen a factor of life and death. Not of far vision, each ox could make out the dark blotch made in the white world by its neighbor.

They did not flee but ran together, and a second croaky blat from Yapao brought them in his direction. At the same time he was moving toward them. As the pioneers of the plains ranged their wagons in a close circle against attacking Indians, so did Yapao, and his herd slowly and cumbrously but with almost human precision gather themselves in a ring of defense. With their backs to a common center they faced outward, and there was just so much space between shoulder and shoulder as though each of the twelve had gone through a manual of training in the matter of this particular formation.

Then, with lowered heads, they waited.

CHAPTER VIII

WITHIN fifty feet of the dark ring of great beasts came Swift Lightning and Mistik, and the big timber-wolf, somewhat appalled by this formidable array of unknown creatures, waited uneasily for the next action of his comrade. Three times Swift Lightning circled about the ring, and the third circle was not more than ten feet from the lowered heads. His body was gathered for a leap-in, and in the beginning of the fourth circle he straightened out like a spring and launched himself straight at Yapao's throat.

But Yapao, though dim of eyesight, saw him coming, and deftly the old warrior swung his shield so that Swift Lightning crumpled up against it with a force that drew an involuntary yelp from him as he was hurled back in the snow. In the same instant there came another thud as Mistik experienced his first encounter with a musk-ox skull. With a snarl Swift Lightning was up and at it again, and the timber-wolf followed bravely. For a space of two or three minutes the thud of their bodies was like a muffled tattoo, and had Yapao and his companions possessed any sense of humor at all the attack of the two wolves would not have been an altogether uninteresting game.

Panting and bruised and with their tongues lolling out, Swift Lightning and Mistik finally drew back a few paces and considered the problem. Round and round Yapao and his crew they circled, but not a head in the ring of defense swerved either to the right or the left, and at last the significance of the situation began to dawn upon Swift Lightning. Until this hour he had never fully realized the necessity of the wolf pack—and it was the pack he needed now.

That the assembling of his comrades was the one and only way of killing the musk-oxen was not a fact deduced by any process of reasoning in his brain, nor was his next action an expression of unusual strategy or quick wit. Just as his animal intelligence told him to call the pack when he struck the trail of a big caribou herd, so now that same intelligence urged him to bring in the killers as quickly as he could.

Running a hundred yards out into the finger of barren he began to howl. He howled as he had never howled before, and Mistik, whose quick perception grasped the importance of the maneuver, continued to snap and feint at the musk-oxen. Even when Swift Lightning had gone so far that his howl came back but faintly, Mistik untiringly stood his guard. As long as the big lone wolf made his circles Yapao had no thought of breaking his battle front.

Three quarters of a mile to the westward the finger of plain that ran through the upheaved tundra opened into the big barren, and straight out into this barren sped Swift Lightning, pausing every few yards to give his call. It had been a long time since the meat-cry of the wolves had swept under the skies, and another mile farther on a lean form, questing hungrily, suddenly stopped and faced its direction. At a far distance a second wolf caught up the signal, and then a third, and as far as there were ears to hear and voices to respond the cry traveled through the night.

In times of the caribou it would have gathered a hundred wolves; tonight, running one by one, thin, red-eyed, and starved, only twelve came to join Swift Lightning. With them he turned back into the curving flat finger of the tundra, and in this ribbon of plain the wolves caught their first scent of the musk-oxen. Mistik was still at his work, and Yapao and his herd were waiting stoically when the pack rushed up out of the gloom.

Now there was real battle under the glow of the stars. Outnumbered by two the heads of Yapao and his crew were no longer motionless, awaiting their turns of assault. Fourteen slashing, swift-leaping, hunger-maddened beasts were at them—and fiercest of all were Swift Lightning and Mistik. Again and again they beat against the head-shields of the musk-oxen. Then came the first snarling howl of animal pain, as one of the killers transfixed himself on Yapao's curving horn. But there was not an instant's halt in the attack. Before Yapao could clear his horn of the wolf a second had buried its fangs in his nose, and in this same moment developed one of those swift and unforeseen happenings which frequently changes the tide of battle. A third wolf, leaping clean over Yapao's bowed neck, was caught on the upswung horn of the ox next to him and in that space both Yapao and his neighbor—burdened under the weight of their transfixed enemies—were unable to protect their part of the defensive ring.

Seizing their advantage with the quickness of the deadliest hunters in the world, half a dozen wolves were at the breach. In a mighty leap one of them shot over the heads to the center of the herd. A second followed him, and the sphinxlike immobility of the herd was gone. The center of it became a trampling and churning mass of destructive hoofs and great bodies.

In perhaps the space of two minutes the life was crushed out of the two wolves. But their sacrifice had broken the herd formation, and the pack swept into the heart of it, lunging at throats and noses. Like sheep the oxen broke now. Yapao himself was on his knees with the big wolf at his nose and Mistik at his throat. Swift Lightning and two others were pulling down a second. In the big beasts there was no fight

when scattered. Hardest of all prey to kill when in
their defensive formation, they were most helpless
when each was dependent upon himself. Their flight
was cumbrous and the terror that possessed them was
the terror of sheep. Yet they were hard to kill because of their long hair and thick wool, and it was
half an hour later before Yapao and two others of the
herd were dead. Of Swift Lightning's pack five out
of the fourteen were killed in the breaking of the ring,
and the nine that were left settled down to a feast that
would have gorged the empty stomachs of fifty.

The silent and mysterious code of intelligences which
spreads over wide areas the news of a "kill" to winged
and clawed things that feed on flesh was already at
work. Hunters—and hunters are those experienced
in the matter—have found themselves baffled in the
explanation of the swiftness and accuracy of its opera-
tion. Where Swift Lightning and Mistik, an hour
before, had found no life in the white and frozen
world about them, there was now, here and there,
manifestation of it.

At first it was only a cautious and starving fox,
peering with his bright little eyes from the edge of
the broken tundra; then an owl, floating silently overhead—from nowhere—disappearing; then a second
fox, and a third; and from dead out of the wind a
bloodthirsty and fearless little ermine, doubling himself
up like a spring at every leap. Within the circle of

these few the scent of warm flesh might easily have carried. But the news traveled beyond. Living things, striking the trails of the fleeing oxen, received the instinctive thrill that the huge beasts were retreating from death; and winged creatures, seeing the flight, knew by that same instinct that slaughter lay behind.

All the hungry things of the barrens evaded the wolf because he was a killer, and yet they followed in his trail because he was the mightiest hunter of them all, and in following him there was hope of the remnants of his feast. And the fox and the ermine and even the owl knew when the wolf was on the trail of prey, and when slaughter was in his cry, just as instinct tells the scavenger crow of the forests to circle above the timber of the swamp out of which has come the shot of a hunter's gun. And tonight there were the trails of twelve wolves that had gathered, and the trails of nine oxen that had fled, and there was also the scent of warm flesh and blood that carried far in the wind.

Glutted for the first time in weeks the wolves did not scatter when they had finished eating, but made themselves burrows in the snow close to the meat or in the edge of the near tundra. The first owl that descended on one of the carcasses was met by a ferocious streak that tore it into pieces before its beak had driven into the flesh, and snarling warnings and mad rushes greeted the foxes who came too near.

If there was an exception, it was Mistik. He, too, was ready to fight for their meat; but over that inclination rode a stronger one—the thing that had been growing steadily in him since his comradeship with Swift Lightning—his desire to go home. And home, for Mistik, meant the big forests and the deep swamps of the country far south. And he wanted Swift Lightning to go with him. Many times he had tried to lure him to it, and tonight he had come nearest to success, for they were heading south as straight as Mistik could go when they struck meat. Now that his hunger was gone and life ran strong in him again he wanted to go on. He whined at Swift Lightning's shoulder and a dozen times trotted across the finger of plain and waited for him to follow, until at last Swift Lightning left the watchful ring of his fellows and joined him.

It was Mistik who led the way. He trotted fast; his ears were aslant; he no longer listened or smelled for game. And on the far edge of the broken tundra, with the great barren sweeping ahead of them again, understanding came to Swift Lightning. He stopped and whined, half turning in the direction from which they had come; and Mistik close at his side, answered that whine—with his face to the south. Off there lay the strange force that was pulling him on, behind them the force that was holding Swift Lightning, and, even as Mistik urged for the forests and the swamps and

the trap-lines of men, Swift Lightning heard again
the call that had drawn him more than once to the
white men's cabin on the edge of the glacier-slash.

He followed Mistik now with a slowness and inde-
cision that made their progress tedious, and at the
end of an hour they were not more than three miles
from the finger of the plain in which they had killed
the musk-oxen. Then it was that the spirit which
rode under the stars of the polar night put its hand
upon him, and across the great plain came its voice—
stopping him, calling to him, demanding of him.

Facing north both Swift Lightning and Mistik listened to that voice. It was the cry of a wolf pack—
the old hunt-cry, the old slaughter-cry, the cry of long
white fang inviting to carnival of feasting and death.
It came to them faintly from the north and west.

And it was not the cry of the seven wolves that
guarded the meat in the slit of plain that ran between
the broken tundra.

In that finger of plain the seven wolves had heard
the approaching cry before it reached Swift Lightning
and Mistik, and in the cry they no longer recognized
the voice of pack-brethren. The near-death of great
hunger, preceded by weeks of fasting and famine, had
wiped out the instinct of brute socialism which was a
part of their living code in times of plenty. For the
time being they were no longer creatures of community
interest but individuals with private property, and in

the defense of that property they were ready to fight against all comers, including those who, only a short time before, had been comrades.

In a scattered group they gathered round the torn carcasses of the three musk-oxen, their fangs gleaming, snarls in their throats, and eyes blazing with the fire of battle as the oncoming pack swept down the slim finger of the plain. It was a small pack, and yet it outnumbered them two to one—an advantage discounted somewhat by the full stomachs of the seven.

Swift Lightning's guard did not move. They waited. A hundred yards away the newcomers halted, and scattering out they advanced slowly, whining hungrily, their jaws clicking in anticipation. They were ready to accept of hospitality, and yet if hospitality were not offered they were prepared to murder. The seven gave no sign or sound of welcome. They stood like carven things and they took no account of number. Had their enemies been fifty instead of fourteen they would still have defended their meat. Their warning carried swiftly to the invading wolves, who were led by Ooyoo, the Howler. It was Ooyoo's howl that had stopped Swift Lightning and Mistik, and it was he who circled nearer than any other of the fourteen, and then darted in toward one of the musk-ox carcasses. The nearest of the seven was at him quick as a flash, and hardly had their bodies met when the thirteen rushed in like shadows driven by a storm.

The six that were left of Swift Lightning's pack met them fang to fang. Meat was forgotten in the rage and blood of battle, and life-and-death struggles were fought over the stiffened bodies of the musk-oxen. Ooyoo, who had leaped in first, died with a torn jugular, so that his blood flooded the glazed eyes of Yapao, the slain king of the herd. In the first fang-slitting rush of battle the seven—well-fed and stronger than their famine-stricken enemies—made a bloody account for themselves.

Wolf to wolf and one at a time they were more than a match for their attackers. But swiftly the weight of numbers began to press upon them. Two of the seven and four of their enemies died so closely about Yapao that their bodies formed a shroud for him. Six of Ooyoo's pack were dead, and three of Swift Lightning's, when the terrible defense turned inevitably to defeat. Gashed and bleeding—four to eight—the defenders slowly gave way, fighting with every foot they retreated. Could the ghost of Yapao have come back then it must have looked on with the triumph of one who has received the full measure of vengeance, for the battle-field was red with blood and close-strewn with dead.

It was in this final bloody moment of the loss of what they themselves had stalked and killed that Swift Lightning and Mistik raced into the edge of the narrow plain. From the instant they first heard the distant howling of the pack they scented battle, and now they leaped into the final act of the tragedy—twin demons shooting straight and swift as bullets.

The twelve wolves were in a twisting mass and into that mass the two gray giants launched themselves. With a single crunch of his jaws Swift Lightning broke the neck of a lean beast whose fangs were buried in another's flesh. Mistik, using his fangs like knives, slashed the throat of a second. Had they come sixty seconds sooner they would have saved the lives of the valiant four who had fought to the last. As it was, two of the four were dead under Ooyoo's horde, and from the throat of a third, even as he fought, ran a stream of blood. But the invaders had paid the price. Only five were left when Swift Lightning found himself battling against two. He was at the throat of one when the second sprang upon him. Together, gripped in a life-and-death duel, the three rolled and twisted in the snow.

Mistik made his second kill and with the last survivor of the seven was in close and deadly combat with the remaining two of Ooyoo's pack.

Swift Lightning, torn and half winded, found himself for the first time outmatched. His own blood was streaming in the snow. As he held to the throat of his enemy the second wolf slashed his sides and rumps, and finally secured a hold at the back of his neck. A sudden terrific agony seized him. The blade of a knife seemed to shoot into his brain, and paralysis, like a stabbing barb of hot iron, closed his eyes and relaxed his jaws. The under wolf, feeling the death-grip at his throat give way, slashed upward quickly and closed on Swift Lightning's under jaw.

Then Swift Lightning put all his remaining strength into a final tremendous effort to free himself. He rolled and twisted his great body, clawing and beating the air, but his jaws were helpless and strength ebbed from him as his brain grew black. Grimly the two wolves hung on. Deeper sank the fangs in Swift Lightning's neck, and death itself was only a moment away when there came a snarling roar, the impact of a giant body—and the paralyzing grip at the base of his brain was gone. Air filled his lungs again, vision returned to his eyes, strength came to his jaws, sound to his ears—and he heard the snarling triumph of Mistik as he slaughtered the foe he had torn from Swift Lightning's neck. He did not wait for the last dying gasp of his enemy but was back again, and his blood-reddened fangs sank deeper into the body of the wolf that held Swift Lightning's jaw.

When Swift Lightning staggered to his feet a few moments later Mistik and the last survivor of the seven were all that were left to keep him company. Vengeance had come to the musk-ox herd, for of one pack of fourteen and another of nine all but these three were dead. Mistik whined softly at Swift Lightning's shoulder, and in that arena of the slain their muzzles touched again and to the intelligence of the beasts was given an understanding of what comradeship had at last meant to them.

CHAPTER IX

FOR many hours after the great fight a storm that was terrible and pitiless in its fury drove off the Arctic Sea. Rushing up over the edge of the earth and hissing over the pole itself, it tore down the shores of Coronation Gulf to empty its venom over the great barrens. It caught up the windrows of the shot-like, frozen particles that were intended for snow and drove them on like canister fired from cannon.

All life burrowed itself out of reach of its fury, for to have faced that storm with its cold of forty degrees below zero meant death. In their igloos the Eskimos hugged tight; the foxes burrowed under the crust of the barren; the wolves curled up in their wallows; the musk-oxen and the caribou close-packed themselves for protection; and even the big white owls with their billows of protecting feathers found shelter for themselves among the dunes and upheavals of the treeless plains.

Swift Lightning lay in a sheltering outcrop of snow and rock, sick with the pain and weakness of his wounds. His body was cut and slashed by the fangs of the wolf horde, and in his brain the wailings of the storm were again the tumult of the starving pack that had attacked his own. In his visions he fought the epic fight again. His jaws snapped weakly, his body quivered, his muscles grew tense, and he heard but little of the storm that raged through the weird black night, blasting the northern world with its fury.

Close beside him lay Mistik. The desire to return to his swamps and his deep timber was still strong upon him. Even in the storm he wanted to go. He tried to rouse Swift Lightning from the stupor that was like sleep. He nudged him with his nose. He whined. He stood up, peering out from their shelter into the black turmoil of the night, wondering why his comrade did not get up and stand beside him. But to all the urgings that rose whimperingly in his throat in the lulls of the wind, Swift Lightning made no response.

Alone in his vigil Mistik watched the hours through. The storm slashed and shrieked itself out. The thunder of it over the barrens grew softer and more distant until at last there was left only a whisper of it in the night. In ones and twos, and then in constellations, the stars came out. Darkness dissolved into starlight, and the mother-of-pearl heart of the sky began to glow in a triumphant illumination. The Aurora, as if rejoicing in the passing of the storm, flung out her glory through the heavens like a dancer flaunting her vivid raiment in the eyes of the world. Curling in and out among the stars, twisting and writhing in a marvelous and sinuous beauty, she shot her ribbons of gold and orange and pale fire like the radiant tresses of a mighty goddess flirting with the blazing hosts of the firmament.

Mistik, seeing the world change marvelously again before his eyes, whined more eagerly. Swift Lightning, coming slowly out of the shadow of the sickness in which he had lain, was conscious that somewhere— far away—Mistik was calling to him. But Mistik did not perceive or understand his effort to answer—the slight tensing of his body, the twitch of his ears, his futile attempt to raise his head. And he went out from the shelter. It seemed to him that he could almost smell his forests, and in the pictures that came and went in his brain he saw them just beyond the edge of the starry horizon. In that brain distance had no mile-stones. One mile, ten, or two hundred—every instinct in his body was urging him to leave this alien country of the starving wolves for his own wide forests and swamps of plenty, where his gray brothers ran.

Slowly he crossed the narrow strip of plain. Twice in three hundred yards he stopped and whined for Swift Lightning to follow him. Again in the broken tundra he paused and waited. And at last on the edge of the great barren that swept out like a sea two hundred miles wide Mistik sat down on his haunches and sent back across the tundra a final yearning cry for Swift Lightning. He listened. And then he turned and headed straight into the south.

Unappalled by distance, and knowing only that his
forests lay somewhere across the white and mysterious
sea, Mistik was going home.

It was the half of a full day after the going of
Mistik that the blinding hand of fever lifted itself
from Swift Lightning's eyes and he raised his head
once more to comprehend the existence of life. Even
then its significance returned to him slowly.

He sensed, first of all, that the big gray timber-wolf
was gone and his first whine was for him. He smelled
of the wallow in which his comrade had lain close
beside him, and it was cold—many hours cold.

After a time he staggered to his feet. He was weak.
He stumbled and limped as he went forth from his
shelter among the dead musk-oxen and wolves. Only
one live wolf was there, snarling and leaping at the
hungry creatures that were preying on the pack's kill.
Swift Lightning took no interest in these starving
things now. He saw snowy owls floating like ghosts
over the bodies and he heard the vicious snapping of
their beaks. Ermine hopped out from under his feet,
and foxes lurked wraith-like in the gloom.

The wolf had exhausted himself in his vain war
against these marauding pests and he looked hopefully
to Swift Lightning for assistance and relief. It did
not enter into his comprehension of things that in the
carcasses of the three musk-oxen and twenty-six wolves
was food for all. Not long ago Swift Lightning would

have fought as he was fighting for the protection of their meat. Now he did not care. He no longer had a desire for meat. His world was changed. Fever and sickness had wrought in him a greater loneliness and a greater yearning than he had ever known before, and for many minutes his questing eyes sought about him for Mistik.

He went back to his shelter and curled himself up in the wallow he had made. Never had his inheritance from the Great Dane pressed upon him more insistently than in this hour of his weakness and his aloneness. His whimper was the whimper of a dog and not of a wolf twenty generations removed from dogs. He wanted companionship in his sickness, and yet the lone wolf could not satisfy his longing. The drop of dog in his blood was like a powerful antitoxin working strangely in the red flood of his savagery. It did not trouble him that the foxes and the ermine and the white owls were gathering to feed on his meat, for when the spirit of Skagen was in him he would have made friends with even the foxes. Not until he was hungry and went out to eat did he disturb them at all.

He found the last trail of Mistik then, and followed it to the edge of the broken tundra, where he stopped and sniffed the air. He did not howl, for something told him what had happened. The trail was cold—and Mistik was gone. For two days and two nights, as the hours would have measured them, he did not go far away. He wandered a little in the narrow plain, sniffing the wind for the sign it might give of Mistik's return. The soreness went from his wounds and the stiffness from his legs.

The third day the wind rose, and Mistik's trail was smothered in the sweepings of the barrens. After that Swift Lightning went no more to the far side of the tundra, but drifted in his aimless questings toward the coast. When he was hungry he returned to the strip of plain that ran like a ribbon through the bad lands, and the memory of starvation faded from his mind. Flesh began to cover his ribs. His magnificent strength returned, yet his loneliness did not leave him, and he still sought for the thing which he could not understand and which he could not find.

Then again the spirit which guides the destinies of the wild set its finger upon him, and a strange thing happened. He was returning from an aimless journey that had taken him twenty miles north and west and had reached the edge of the bad land in the heart of which was the frozen meat, when a sudden shifting of the wind brought him to the rigidity of a rock. In that wind came both scent and sound—scent that thrilled him, and sound that drove new heat into every drop of blood in his body. The smell was of man. The sound was of howling dogs far away. Through his body surged again the ferocity of the wolf, for the smell and the sound were coming straight from the meat on which for a week he had fed and grown strong. He advanced into the wind to the edge of the tundra and looked out over the strip of plain.

In the vivid starlight he no longer saw the lone wolf or the foxes or the floating owls. Close to where Yapao had fallen was a line of dogs and a long sledge, and beyond that was another string of dogs and another sledge. Between these two sledges furred and hooded creatures were at work swiftly and excitedly, and the clacking of their tongues came to Swift Lightning in a ceaseless chatter.

Eskimo hunters had found what was left of the dead musk-oxen and wolves. Never had they made a luckier find, for in this winter of famine the Great Hunger was upon man as well as beast. Upi, the big hunter of his village, was chanting in his joy as he cut and slashed at the frozen meat, and the five Eskimos with him worked like fiends. With an ax, for which Upi had traded his wife to the captain of a whaling-ship earlier in the winter, they chopped up the carcasses of the oxen. Now and then one of them paused to send the long lash of a whip over the backs of the excited and famished dogs.

Crouched on his belly, and hardly breathing as he watched, Swift Lightning looked upon the spoliation of his meat for which he had sacrificed his pack and almost his life.

The work of the Eskimos was done quickly. In

another half-hour, shouting and cracking their whips, they started their teams out through the neck of the finger of plain. For a long time Swift Lightning listened to them. After the sound of their whips had died away he could still hear their wild and exultant shouts, the savage and far-reaching pæans of their joy.

Not until the last of their voices was gone did he go out into the open where the meat had been. From somewhere the wolf joined him. The foxes slunk out into the edge of the plain, and the big owls floated overhead again. All that was left were the chips of frozen flesh made by the cutting of the ax. Of these Swift Lightning made a last meal.

When he had finished he started out slowly and cautiously over the trail of the Eskimo hunters. Neither desire nor reason directed his movements. He felt no rage at his loss, and no thought of vengeance on man or beast entered into his action. The trail drew him on even as he sensed its peril. Its lures hypnotized him into movement directly contrary to the instinct which told him he was playing with fire. His mind was pulled and urged by a series of paradoxical phenomena, the forces that urged him on being stronger than those that pulled him back.

As he followed he was in many ways neither wolf nor dog. Like some humans "born wrong" he was a misfit in the world of which he was a part. Not long ago he had found a keen joy in running under the light of the stars and the glow of the aurora. Now that joy was gone, and he would have shunned the wolf pack even as he avoided a closer contact with the peril of men and dogs.

No psychology of his own could have revealed the mystery of these things to him, and yet the brain of a white man—watching him and knowing the fact of his birth—would have solved easily the inexplicable. The heritage of the dog was now upon Swift Lightning, *and his soul was lonely for that thing which it had never known and could not understand.*

CHAPTER X

FOR many hours the Eskimos traveled with their treasures north and west, and now and then Swift Lightning approached near enough to hear the howling of the dogs and the shouting of men. A sun would have risen and set before they reached the village.

Half a mile away, in a summit of ice, Swift Lightning heard the exultation and triumph of their homecoming. In the wind came the smell as well as the voice of the village. The smell he did not like. It was human and not like the smell of animals, tainting his nostrils and distasteful in his mouth—a potpourri of exhalations that freighted the air unpleasantly. It was not like the scent that had come from the white men's cabin on the edge of the glacier-slash, and he shunned it, traveling round the village to the ice of the sea.

Now that he had struck the coast he kept on still westward. His vision reached for half a mile over the polar ice, and a vague impulse drew him out upon it. The great fields lay white and glistened softly, sending back to the sky a silvery illumination, so that between sea and heaven hung a radiant mist of light. It was so quiet that the click of Swift Lightning's claws rattled like tiny castanets as he trotted. Frequently he stopped and found himself puzzled by the shifting of the air.

After a time he gave up trying to keep in the face of the wind, and because of this an unusual thing happened. Half a dozen miles from the Eskimo village and a mile from the shore a ghost rose up out of the night ahead of him, and he had not smelled it. It fitted in so illusively with the silvery mist that he was close upon it before discovery, and with a startled snap of his jaws he stopped short.

What he saw was a ship—a ghost-white ship smothered in ice, with skeleton arms reaching up to the sky. Never had he seen a thing like it before. It was deadly still. It sent him slinking back, and he gathered himself with the wind in a wide and questing circle.

Then it came to him—the scent. His eyes blazed with a strange fire for it was the scent of the white men's cabin. Yet this that he saw was not a cabin. Then came the miracle. There was light! He saw again the flame-made glow of a sun, and he heard sound—a man's harsh voice and the yelp of a kicked dog. Silence fell after that. On the ship men's lives were guided by the hands of a clock; it was night and they were sleeping.

Three times he circled round the ship, approaching

a little nearer with each circuit, and the third time he squatted on his haunches. After a little he threw back his head and sent forth his cry, and in the stillness of the night it seemed to rise to the farthest stars. The last of it had not left his throat when pandemonium broke loose aboard the ship. A score of Eskimo dogs answered the call. Their cries roused the sleeping men, and the voice Swift Lightning had heard before came again, cursing and condemning, as the heart of the malamute chorus was broken by other howls and the lashing of a whip, that cut the night like the reports of a pistol.

Swift Lightning trotted back cautiously. All that sound held menace. He did not go hastily but made wide circles as he retreated; and in making one of these circles his nose struck a trail. He ran over it and then stopped. It was in a bit of soft snow sheltered by an upheaval of ice, and its scent was quite plain. It was not fox, it was not wolf, and it was not Eskimo dog. *And yet it was dog!* But the difference between this scent and all others that he had ever known thrilled Swift Lightning as nothing had ever thrilled him before. Its mystery held him rigid for many minutes. He breathed it in deeply. He held his nose in the imprints of the feet that had made it, and his body pulsed in a sudden marvelous awakening. Ahead of him, running alone, was a creature whose existence filled his soul with new desire. It crept upon him insistently, calling to him and urging him. And he followed.

The footprints led him back to the land. There, a mile from the ship, rose up before him a grim and ghostly cairn of rocks, and out of the cairn a leaden slab on which was written:

SACRED TO THE MEMORY OF JOHN BRAINE
OF THE SMITHSONIAN INSTITUTION
DIED, JANUARY 4, 1915.

"Thus saith the Lord of Hosts;
Consider your ways."
Haggai, Chap. 1, 5, 7.

But the cairn and the slab meant nothing to him. They impressed themselves upon him more than other things simply because the footprints of the creature he was following were very numerous about them and the scent was stronger. Here and there were smooth places where Firefly, the collie, had come to lie beside the grave of her master. Only that master, out of the sacred memories that had died with him, could have told what the name and the heart of a dog had held for him—for it was a woman who had named the collie "Firefly," and thousands of miles away it was a woman who was waiting and praying for them—for the one that was masterless and the other who was dead.

Swift Lightning circled round the cairn, smelled of

it, and put his forefeet high upon it so that he could touch the leaden slab with his nose. And the dead man's dog had done this same thing. She had raised herself up to the slab many times so that her claw-marks were on the stones and in the snow. Swift Lightning found where she had lain beside her master last. There were yellow hairs in the wallow, and the scent of it was quite fresh compared with the others. Slowly he picked up her fresh trail as it went away from the cairn. It did not return to the ship but headed up the shore, and half a mile away was a paw-beaten spot in the snow where Firefly had stood for many minutes as if in great doubt. Twice from this point she had set out as if to return to the ship, but each time had changed her mind. She went on straight away from both the ship and the cairn.

For an hour Swift Lightning followed her trail, making no great effort to overtake her—yet he knew that with each step he was drawing nearer. It was a wandering trail and always westward. It nosed in and out among great hummocks of snow and ice, and only in the open spaces did it lead on without hesitation. Frequently it was marked by the paw-beaten spots where Firefly had stopped. A hunter, knowing the tracks to be those of a dog, would have said that she was lost or that she was seeking something. For it was a questing trail—the trail of a dog seeking its master or its home.

Three or four miles from the cairn the level of the barren ended at the edge of a mighty deposit of glacial ice. With his caution and his instinctive shunning of the sea Swift Lightning would have turned inland, but the collie's trail swung in the opposite direction and brought him straight to the edge of the frozen ocean. Here again it swung westward. He quickened his pursuit. The scent of Firefly's paws was warm in the trail now, and he began to trot, the whine in his throat trembling with anticipation as he watched ahead of him.

And then he saw her. She stood on the crest of a little knoll of clear ice not fifty feet away from him, facing the sea. The glow of the moon and stars seemed to concentrate itself in a soft spotlight about her. She was standing sideways, a slim, beautiful creature with long gold-yellow hair that gave to her body a silken shimmer. Her head was poised, listening and watchful, and facing the sea.

Swift Lightning paused. In all his life he had seen nothing like this dog from a woman's home two thousand miles away, and even as his body remained as if carven out of rock the yearning of his soul escaped him in a low whine.

Quick as a flash Firefly turned her head. Swift Lightning whined again and advanced hesitantly, as if entreating for an invitation. On her pinnacle of ice Firefly gave no response. Her eyes shone. Gold-yellow and shimmering softly she waited, inviting him, luring him, yet making no sound.

Ten seconds more and he stood under her, every instinct of courtship swelling in him. His crest stood up. He pranced as he whined, his splendid head was erect, and his body seemed moved by springs instead of muscles. His magnificence forced itself upon the beautiful and masterless creature above him, and her glowing eyes followed every movement he made.

Then Swift Lightning heard her low whine answering him. It was a whimper of unutterable loneliness, a plea for friendship, an answer to his message.

His heart throbbed joyously. Between him and Firefly lay the steep ten-foot ascent of smooth ice, and in his excitement he made an heroic effort to climb it. Fiercely he dug in his toe-nails, and foot by foot he scrambled up until he was almost at the top. Then he slipped, and in slipping lost his balance and somersaulted to the bottom with a force that knocked a grunt out of him.

He picked himself up sheepishly and looked away from Firefly nonchalantly, as if nothing had happened. Then he trotted round the end of the ice hummock and found where Firefly herself had climbed to her pedestal. It was an easy ascent.

When he reached the top she was waiting for him, flat on her belly, her head between her forepaws; and for perhaps half a minute Swift Lightning stood over her, not once looking down but out over the empty sea. Yet he was seeing nothing, looking for nothing.

There was an almost audible throb of exultation in his body in these moments of triumph. It was difficult for him to keep his dignity. He wanted to jump and bark and caper about and make a fool of himself. But for a space he held his pose. Then, slowly, he looked down. Firefly was watching him from between her yellow paws. Never had he seen a wolf's eyes like hers. They were not shifting. They looked at him steadily, deep pools of softness. And something about her *talked* to him. He bent his head. His muzzle touched the silken softness of the long yellow hair on her neck—and then it touched her nose. A soft sound rose in Firefly's throat. It was answered in his.

Through twenty generations of wolves Swift Lightning had at last come into possession of his own.

It was hours later, still other miles to the west, that Swift Lightning and Firefly came to the end of the glacial ice. They had not traveled fast, and Swift Lightning had given up all thought of leadership. Firefly had quickly dispossessed him of that. With the tact and efficiency of her sex in such matters she had assumed to a large extent the prerogative of selecting the trails in which they should travel, and swelling with the happiness of matehood Swift Lightning sensed the fact that he should not be ungentlemanly enough to argue matters with her in these first hours of their honeymoon. So where Firefly went he followed. It was a delightful change for him, yet instinctively he felt its dangers, for Firefly was as much a stranger in this savage world of his as he would have been in the alleys of a big city.

She was sublimely unconscious of her limitations. Sleek and shimmering and beautiful she had never known the pangs of starvation. She did not know that to live amid this desolation of ice and snow necessitated the watchfulness of the hunter at every step. Aboard the ship she had known only two perils—the menace of the wild malamute dogs and the "gentlemen in the white jackets"—the polar bears. A wounded bear had almost killed her, and thereafter she regarded the white monsters as the most dreaded of all living things. But the bear had come up out of the sea, and here she was on solid footing.

She turned at last into the mouth of a giant crack in the wall, a crevasse that was like a narrow chasm running into the heart of the ice mountain. Here Swift Lightning made an effort to call her back. Instinct told him to avoid those traps. But after hesitating for a moment Firefly gave him to understand that if he did not want to follow she would go on alone. He trotted to her good-humoredly, though his presentiment of evil did not leave him. The floor of the crevasse was like an up-hill trail, and they climbed steadily for two or three hundred yards before they stopped again.

Moonlight filled the chasm. It glistened on the ice walls and the frozen crags towering far above their heads, and its reflection between those shimmering walls was the radiance of a pale sun. But Swift Lightning was unconscious of its beauty, oblivious to the wonder of it. As they stood there presentiment was giving way to suspicion—suspicion to the knowledge of a slow and approaching reality.

When Firefly made as if to go on he whined, and there was a new note in that whine. It stopped her. It sent her sleek head erect as the message sped from Swift Lightning to her that something was coming up the chasm.

For a full minute they stood without moving and in that minute they heard sound—a slow *click, click, click* as though someone were tapping the ice with a metal rod, and a moment later full in their vision came Wapusk, the big polar bear. Until he appeared over a steep crest in the floor of the crevasse Swift Lightning did not get the full scent of him. It was not alone a polar-bear scent. It was a *particular* scent— the strong, musky odor of the bear he had fought at the Eskimo igloo many days ago. And Firefly, seeing Wapusk, recognized the creature she feared more than all other things on earth.

Wapusk smelled his prey close at hand, and stopped. He was a bad bear, a cannibal, a human-flesh-eating monster in the days of his fight with Swift Lightning at the igloo. But he was worse now. The barb of an Eskimo spear was buried in his shoulder. It had lamed him and had made him still more ferocious. And again Swift Lightning heard the low and ominous roll of thunder in his throat. He responded with a snarl, and with that snarl came Firefly's whimper of terror.

She was no longer the proud and triumphant female, but pressed close against Swift Lightning, in this hour her master, her mate, her protector, against all other things.

As he had sensed the futility of open battle at the igloo, Swift Lightning sensed it now. Only one way of possible escape lay before them—a retreat still farther up the narrowing crevasse. There was no alternative.

He turned, but not in a panic. With a thrust of his shoulder he headed Firefly, and she began to trot, and then, as he set the pace himself, to run.

They heard behind them the clatter of Wapusk's long claws, and the sound sent Firefly's body like a yellow streak through the moonlight. The crevasse grew narrower and rougher. And then, all at once, they came to the end of it. On three sides of them the ice walls rose a hundred feet high, precipitous, and unbroken. Swift Lightning took in the situation. He knew that again he was facing death. His eyes sought for a crack or a mass of ice from which he might defend himself and Firefly. Then he saw at the farther side of the crevasse a dark shadow that gave him hope. He ran to it with Firefly at his shoulder. The shadow was made by a flat ledge in the ice wall about six feet above the level of the crevasse floor. It was a last refuge—a last hope.

Running back fifteen or twenty feet, he turned in a mighty leap that carried him to the ledge. It was his only way of telling Firefly what to do, and now he whined down to her, entreating her to jump before it was too late. The clatter of Wapusk's claws on the ice came nearer—and desperately Firefly made the effort. She struck two feet under the ledge and fell back with a whimper of terror and pain. A second time she reached the edge of the ledge so that for a space she clung to it, fighting to raise herself up. Again she slipped back, and out of Swift Lightning came a snarl of rage as he saw Wapusk's huge body coming swiftly toward them. He prepared himself to leap.

Another twenty seconds and he would have launched himself at the bear in a last great fight. In those seconds fear and the nearness of death put into Firefly the strength for a last effort, and she shot once more for the ledge. Two-thirds of her body reached it, and with a sudden grip of his teeth in her hair Swift Lightning helped her the rest of the way.

They were not an instant too soon. A monster paw struck where Firefly's golden body had been, and then the full eight feet of Wapusk reared itself to the face of the ledge. Swift Lightning drove straight at his nose, and Wapusk's roar of pain and fury rumbled in a hundred echoes along the walls and in the caverns of ice. Flattened against the barrier ten feet away Firefly watched the defense of her mate and master.

There was a new fire in her eyes. They were like flaming diamonds. She had been a petted and fondled creature, but the fighting blood of the collie was in her. And in these moments it was Swift Lightning —and Swift Lightning alone—that filled her whole world. The great white arms of Wapusk reached out like human things. She saw one of them strike, with Swift Lightning under it. Then the arm crooked itself about his body, and without a sound she shot in to the rescue. Her teeth, sharp as needles, sank to the gums in Wapusk's furry paw, and the arm straightened and a roar such as had never come out of his chest before came from Wapusk. For Firefly, striking in a blind fury, had found the tenderest spot in all his fifteen-hundred-pound body.

Bleeding and half crushed Swift Lightning sprang back, and Firefly leaped with him. They ran to the end of the ledge as Wapusk pulled himself up, and here—their final salvation—was a crack four feet wide in the ice mountain. Swift Lightning drove Firefly in ahead of him, and Wapusk was at the mouth of the crack by the time they were ten feet in. The crack narrowed so quickly that in another twenty feet Wapusk's great body could proceed no farther, and furious growls of disappointment echoed to the heart of the frozen mountains.

Up and up through that narrow crack continued Firefly and Swift Lightning until they came out on the great glacial plateau at the top. They were high above the sea and high above the plain. Down to the barrens ran the landward slope of the glacier. About them the world lay in a glory of moonlight and starlight, and with a whimper that might have been a prayer of gratitude and thankfulness Swift Lightning dropped down on his belly at the edge of a scarp of ice and looked forth into that world. Close to him Firefly laid herself down, her warm, soft body against him, in her throat a low whimper trembling with the mystery of understanding, of promise and of a birthright at last fulfilled. And then, very gently, her warm tongue began to nurse the bleeding wound in Swift Lightning's shoulder.

And Swift Lightning, still looking out into the barrens, saw no more the loneliness and emptiness and cold desolation of his world. For through twenty generations of wolves his heritage had come to him. The spirit of the Great Dane had triumphed at last. The miracle had happened, and his world was changed forever.

CHAPTER XI

MIGHTIEST of all nature's forces—mightier than flood and storm—hollowers of valleys, levelers of mountains, sculptors that have chiseled the features of continents are the glaciers. Their appointed task is done. In the ages that have passed they have crept over the face of the earth, slow and implacable, irresistible as the swing of the sphere in their orbits, fashioning an abiding-place for the feet of men. They have dug their lakes and their rivers; they have pounded and crushed and mixed the earth's strata; they have directed forever the flow of waters. Splendidly they have played their part as the last great working force of God in His magnificent achievement of Creation.

On the edge of the polar sea, its mission restricted now to contributing millions of tons of icebergs to the ocean each summer, lay Ussisooi—the Ice Chisel—a great, flat, slowly moving mountain of ice giving up grudgingly its last precious secrets to the ocean.

The sea face of Ussisooi was broken and cracked and filled with great caverns and deep fissures; in summer storms the tides roared in it with a voice of thunder, and crags and mountains of ice broke off with terrific explosions and floated away to sea.

But back of this ragged and fighting sea edge, and at its top, Ussisooi was level as a table.

It was a white man's dog—a white *woman's* dog—that stood at Swift Lightning's side on the top of Ussisooi. With the beauty of blood and breed in every line of her graceful body she was the living and breathing embodiment of the dreams and strange yearnings that had made Swift Lightning unlike all his brethren of the wolf packs.

Her memories were still vivid. Only yesterday, it seemed, she had felt the caress of a woman's soft white hands thousands of miles south—a woman in whose face there was grief and yet pride, sorrow and yet love—on that day when the master had taken her away on the big ship. Of the woman, Firefly thought only as one thinks of a great desire. She was living, waiting, calling—*somewhere off there!*

She stood with her shoulder against Swift Lightning's. In the soft whimpering of her voice were longing and uncertainty, and the gentle throat sounds she made tensed his muscles to the hardness of steel. This was *his* world. He understood it, and he knew that to live in it meant to fight. All his life he had fought—and killed. And he wanted to fight something again—*now!* The desire boiled in his blood. He was fired by the heroic inspirations of a young gallant escorting a timid and pretty girl through a rough crowd. In the overwhelming exuberance of these first hours of his honeymoon he wanted to show himself off. And in his environment the one best way to "show off" was to kill something. He was not satisfied with his defensive fight against Wapusk. So he pranced a few yards away from Firefly, his head erect, his crest like a brush, his step springy and challenging.

"Take a look at me, Firefly," he seemed to say. "I'm not afraid of anything on earth—not even Wapusk. I can lick any wolf that ever walked. I can run farther and faster than any other wolf in the world. If you say so I'll go back and lick Wapusk himself!"

And Firefly looked. She was fascinated by this savage and magnificent beast who paraded before her. She ran to him and yipped approvingly and stared with him off into nothingness.

The blood swelled in Swift Lightning's veins. Why couldn't something turn up, he wondered. He ran back to the crack up which they had crawled to the top of Ussisooi and snarled. Right then he would have welcomed the appearance of the great bear himself.

But Wapusk at that very moment was having a time of his own. Even as Swift Lightning and Firefly stood at the edge of the fissure they heard a pandemonium of sound from the far end of the glacier—the howling of dogs, human yells, and the roaring of the bear. For a moment or two Swift Lightning listened. Then he flattened his ears and set off at a trot toward the sounds, whining for Firefly to follow him. They had covered two or three hundred yards when the surface of the Ice Chisel began to slope toward the sea. Down this slope Swift Lightning went more cautiously until he came to the sharp edge of a precipitous fall of fifty or sixty feet. Firefly crowded against him and they looked down.

Out of the starlit and moon-filled cup of the glacier below them rose a hideous turmoil of battle. They could see the fighters distinctly—the great white form of Wapusk, a dozen dogs, and the swiftly moving shadows of Eskimo hunters. Forgetting his yearning for an opportunity to display his own prowess Swift Lightning instinctively crouched flat on his belly. Firefly stood up, clearly outlined against the rim of the glacier top, paralyzed by what she saw. There were three men shrieking and yelling and darting in and out among the attacking malamutes, the steel points of their long spears flashing like silver arrows. Wapusk, with the wall of the ice mountain behind him, was putting up a tremendous fight.

One of the hunters leaped in. A spear flashed, and Wapusk swung toward the enemy who had made the thrust. In that off-guard moment a second figure closed in, and a still deadlier stroke caught the bear back of his giant shoulder.

Wapusk rose and flung himself among the dogs. He had ceased to roar. Choking sounds filled his throat.

A killer all his life, a wanderer on land, an eater even of human flesh, retribution at last had fallen upon him. With fresh spears the Eskimos closed in, and he struck blindly and weakly. Then came the moment when he no longer swept aside the dogs. He rolled over. The sounds in his throat died away, and using the shafts of their spears as clubs the hunters drove the dogs away from him. Wapusk was dead.

During the fight below her Firefly had hardly seemed to breathe. In her brain the visions and memories of another world were dissolving into the grim realities of the present. Even on the ship she had been sheltered and petted. And now she beheld death under the stars and the moon.

Looking up, one of the hunters saw her silhouetted against the sky. In their excitement even the dogs had not noticed her. The hunter stopped. Then he stood up; his arm swung back, shot forward, and one of the shimmering assagai-like spears hissed through the air. The steel barb of it struck the ice a dozen inches under Firefly's feet. That much higher and it would have pierced her. The ring of the steel, the fall of the shaft, and the movement below roused her instantly to a sense of danger and she sprang back. In the same moment Swift Lightning joined her and led her away at a trot.

What they had witnessed was not a tragedy to him. It was merely a killing, the most common of all

happenings in this world of his. He did not feel Firefly's emotions for he was neither afraid nor shocked.
He was disappointed. There had been a fight, just
the sort of thing he had been yearning for, and it had
been impossible for him to play a part in it. That
was the distressing thing to him about Wapusk's death.
As they left the sea edge of Ussisooi farther and farther behind them, he swelled again with the desire to
impress upon this beautiful mate of his some proof of
his splendid prowess.

In this humor he led Firefly to the landward edge of
the glacier.

On this side the ice mountain sloped down to the
barrens—a long, straight hill of smooth ice probably
three or four hundred feet from top to bottom. Or-
dinarily he would have been most cautious here but
tonight he was a very devil in his disdain for possible
mishaps and pranced up to the treacherous edge as
though Ussisooi herself would dare to play him no
trick. To Firefly the shimmering slope appeared inno-
cent enough. There was nothing about it that alarmed
her; it looked quite easy to descend.

And then the thing happened. Swift Lightning's
forefeet slipped. The front part of his body shot out
from under him and for a matter of seconds he hung
on desperately with his hind claws. Then, an inch at
a time, he gave way—and under Firefly's startled and
wondering eyes he started on his undignified journey.

For a dozen yards or so he slipped like a sled; then a knob in the ice pivoted him sideways so that he lost his balance utterly, and from that moment he had no clear comprehension of what was happening to him. The last thing he saw was Firefly looking down at him from the edge of Ussisooi. For three hundred feet or more he rolled and twisted and somersaulted, gathering greater speed as his journey continued. He shot over "falls" in the ice slope, and the wind was knocked out of him. At times he rode on his back, at others on his nose, and at still others he was whirling head over heels in the air.

When he reached the bottom he was like a sack of wheat clubbed out of shape. He stood up groggily. He was dizzy. There was a strange turning-round of things in his stomach. But he was not blind—and what he saw brought him to his senses and to immediate if unsteady action. His plunge down the ice mountain had landed him full in the midst of a bunch of arctic hares. The big white creatures were stunned by his sudden appearance. Perhaps they thought him a chunk of ice. Before they learned he was alive he had one of them in his jaws.

His body, trained to certain things, had acted like a mechanical device, and he had caught the hare instinctively. Now, as his brain cleared, the presence of the dead hare for the first time began to have a significance. Into Swift Lightning's quick wit leaped

the inspiration that the thing he had killed might be
laid at Firefly's feet as an apology for his sudden and
undignified descent. His pride and his dignity were
upset, but his spirits returned as he rose more steadily
to his feet with the big white rabbit between his jaws.
He would return with it to Firefly. He would let her
understand it was for *that* he had made his spectacular
descent down Ussisooi. He trotted to the edge of
the icy slope—and there suddenly he stopped. Again
his plans went to smash. He heard sounds—a terrified
"Yip, yip, yip!"—and he knew Firefly was coming
down to him.

The hare dropped from his jaws. He stood motionless as the ice itself. He heard her before he saw her—
her frightened yipping, the pummeling and scraping
of her body, a frenzied howl as she went over the first
of the ice falls. Then he saw her. She was descending
like a huge yellow tenpin ball, and when she reached
bottom—and whizzed past him—Swift Lightning
grabbed up the hare and trotted toward her. Firefly,
gaining her feet, was going round and round in a
groggy circle.

Swift Lightning pranced just outside that circle.

"See here, Firefly," he seemed to say. "This rabbit
is what I came down for. I got it for you."

As she steadied herself he danced up to her. The
next half-minute was the busiest half-minute of all
his life. Without waiting to view the matter from any

other angle but the present one Firefly lighted into him, and in those thirty seconds Swift Lightning received the very strong impression that he was being massacred.

Yet he was not much hurt. Some of his hair was pulled out, but Firefly's upbraiding was, in fact, nine-tenths vocal and only one-tenth bite; so that, when the thing was over, Swift Lightning was still of the impression that he had received a healthy drubbing yet did not feel the hurt of it. Not once had he struck back. In his amazement and helplessness he had not even dropped his rabbit.

These facts, at the end of the thirty seconds, were taken stock of by Firefly. She stood back and looked at him. Swift Lightning, with the big hare in his mouth, faced her patiently. The growl in her throat softened. She looked away from him—then back. Swift Lightning wriggled his body. Firefly deigned to wag her beautiful tail just a trifle. All at once, she ran to him and thrust her muzzle against his neck. And then, forgetting what had happened, they feasted together on the flesh of Wapoos, the hare.

CHAPTER XII

THROUGH these wonderful first hours of their matehood there was no method to the wanderings of Swift Lightning and Firefly. It was not until she began to grow tired that a definite objective formed itself in Firefly's mind. The great plains thrilled her, and whenever she paused to gaze ahead and listen it was not the sea she faced but always the south—the direction of the forests, of the sun, of warmth and light and home. But exhaustion turned her the other way and roused in her the homing instinct that recalled her to the cairn of stones and the ship.

No sooner had she headed toward them than Swift Lightning sensed what was impending. He knew that the cairn and the ship were vitally associated with her existence, and he resented them. Instinct warned him that he might lose her if she returned to the ship.

Firefly, on the other hand, regarded the situation from an entirely different view-point. There were things on the ship which she hated, and she hated them more than ever now that her master was gone. Especially the wild malamute dogs. But for many months the ship had been her home. Food and warmth were there, a comfortable bed, long hours in which to sleep.

And she knew no reason why Swift Lightning should not return to these things with her. She had no intention of leaving him behind and she had her own feminine methods of persuasion. At times when Swift Lightning held back she whimpered and whined and coaxed him until he proceeded again; at others, when her cajolery failed to budge him, she set off deliberately by herself—as if to give him up for good—and in a panic of apprehension he would very soon overtake her.

In this way they came at last to the cairn of rocks. And here, in one of the many wallows already made by her body, Firefly lay down.

Swift Lightning lay beside her. It seemed to him that she was listening for some sound from out of the cairn, and he, too, listened. For many minutes she lay watchful and intent. Then she rose from the wallow and trotted toward the sea. Swift Lightning followed her to the ice and there he stopped.

After that, a little at a time, Firefly urged him on. He was not the old Swift Lightning now. There was no longer the proud and defiant poise to his head and the springiness was gone from his step. Firefly was going back to her home—the ship. He heard men's voices and the odor of dogs came to him. In a last effort he tried to tell her this was the dead-line beyond which he could not go. And still Firefly did not understand. She entreated him. Three times she trotted on ahead of him, and three times she returned to where he lay motionless in the snow, his nose straight out between his forepaws. Then a fourth time she left him, and this time did not return.

Swift Lightning waited—waited until his body was stiff with the cold and the last spark of his hope was gone. Slowly he turned shoreward. Again it was his old world that lay about him. The beauty and the thrill of the night were gone. Once more it was a gray and empty chaos of gloom, a vast space filled with maddening loneliness. Never had this loneliness pressed upon him as in this hour—like a physical weight, like a thing crushing out all hope and desire from his soul. The Cree, wise in the tragic passing of his years, says that God was right in not giving to the beasts the power of reason, for with reason they would have exterminated men from the face of the earth—and it was that reason which Swift Lightning lacked now. Tomorrow, the next day, or the day after held no meaning for him except as they existed in the present hour. And the present was black with the hopelessness of despair.

He returned to the cairn and lay down in the wallow last warmed by Firefly's golden body. He was tired; yet in her company he had not felt exhaustion. For many hours he had traveled without rest before he came upon the ship and her trail, and for many hours after that he had traveled with her. For more than a day and a night his splendid muscles had labored without sleep, and now sheer tiredness overcame him. He fought against it. He did not want to sleep. His mental desire was to remain awake and watchful that he might not miss Firefly should she return over the ice. A dozen times he stirred himself before he fell at last into uneasy slumber.

It was a sleep filled with restless and swiftly changing dreams. When he awoke several hours later a heavy gloom had settled over the white earth and sea. The stars were hidden. The aurora was dead. Round the crest of the cairn moaned a bit of wind—a sobbing, heart-choking breath of wind—as though the soul of the woman had come to weep over its dead.

Swift Lightning circled in the direction of the ship. Out on the open ice the wind, sweeping low over its fields, bit at him fiercely. It was a snow-rolling wind, driving thick volleys of shot-like drift into his eyes and nostrils, shutting out both vision and scent. In such a wind, with its playful piling up of ridges and dunes, it was impossible to trail and useless to hunt. Yet on this night it was a friend to Swift Lightning. Instinct told him that he was safe no matter how close he went to the ship. For it is brute instinct to sense and feel danger only when it can be heard by the ears, scented through the nose, or seen with the eyes.

Stopping every few steps to sniff and listen he made his way slowly round the ship, and on the opposite side came to the ice-bridge that sloped up from the surface

of the sea to the deck of the vessel. Up and down this
bridge traveled the feet of the men and beasts that belonged to the whaler; up its hard-beaten surface were
dragged the flesh and skins of slain bears and seals;
down it went the hunter and the trader. And no matter how fiercely the wind-brooms of the night swept
it they could not take away all of its scents. These
scents Swift Lightning drank in a little at a time. And
in his soul, fighting between the mastery of the wolf
and the dog, there worked slowly a strange and wonderful transmutation. *He wanted to go up!* He
wanted to go where Firefly had gone. He wanted to
climb to the top of that man-made trail!

And then, in this hour when he might have gone on
a little farther, the wind fell dead with a sleepy sigh,
the clouds drifted away, and the unveiled moon flooded
the sea with light so suddenly that it was like a gigantic
flare. Over and about him Swift Lightning saw what
the frolicsome trickery of the wind had concealed for
a space—the great dark hull, the weird, white-frozen
masts and spars, and in that same instant, so near that
astonishment seized upon them both, a thing that was
life.

The thing was a man. He stood not two good leaps
away, looking down from the top of the bridge, his
face white in the moonlight, his eyes staring. It was
Bronson, caretaker of the dogs aboard ship—Bronson,
nicknamed the "white Eskimo" because, of his forty

years, he had spent twenty in the arctic. He slipped
back swiftly and ran to the kennels of snow and ice
on the far side of the ship where the dogs were chained.

Swift Lightning heard the faint clink of frosty
steel as he moved out upon the ice. Scent and sound
were very clear to him now, and he smelled both men
and dogs. He heard the movement of dogs, and with
that movement the *clink, clink, clink* of the chains.
But he did not run. He was not afraid, and in him
flared up a sudden fire of hatred for the beasts that
were making the chains clink. In him were bred
deeply the "to have and to hold" laws of the pack—
its passions of matehood, of rivalry, and of terrific
fighting; and in the smell of the dogs he felt the reason
for Firefly's desertion of him. His great loneliness
and his yearning of a few minutes before were submerged in the fury of jealousy that raged through him.
Sullenly he trotted away from the ship for a couple
of hundred yards.

There were eight of Bronson's "bear-teasers" that
came down the ice bridge—eight lithe-bodied, long-
legged, deep-jowled Airedales that had been taught to
hold silence and to hang by the ears without yelping.
It took them less than a dozen seconds to pick up Swift
Lightning's scent and to comprehend the business ahead
of them.

At the edge of a snow hummock crouched Swift
Lightning. Less than twenty feet separated him from

the onrushing pack when he shot out with the swiftness of an arrow, striking at the leading dog as he would have struck at a caribou. With the force of a hundred-and-forty-pound rock he landed against the shoulder of the sixty-pound Airedale, and in that same instant his jaws closed, and Bronson's best fighter gave scarcely a gasp as his neck snapped in the first mad fury of Swift Lightning's vengeance.

A quarter of a minute more and he was the center of a furious, snarling, slashing mass of dogs. Instead of fighting him as Eskimo dogs or other wolves would have fought, the seven Airedales piled on him as they would have pyramided themselves over a cat. Sheer force of weight and number bore him down, and because of seven crowding bodies seeking blindly to annihilate him Swift Lightning fought at an enormous advantage. His jaws closed on forelegs that snapped like sticks; his long teeth slashed upward and sideways into the bellies of his enemies; and with every roll and twist he found flesh and blood for his fangs.

The sound of battle carried to the ship. Bronson, armed with a seal spear, was running toward the fight. A window flared with light. Other dogs howled and a score of malamutes who had been sleeping heavily in their snow wallows a few minutes before uncurled themselves, stood up, and then raced to join the combat.

It did not occur to Swift Lightning that his personal affair had become a matter of more or less exciting import to the entire ship. He was fighting blindly and furiously at the bottom of the pile of dogs. Over the backs of the fighters rose a vaporish exhalation like a mist. He felt the rake and slash of teeth. They slit into his flanks and ripped at his sides, and twice they sank deep into his neck. Then a second of Bronson's dogs was out of the fight for good, and Swift Lightning had a chest hold on a third when the malamute dogs began streaming into the mêlée.

Now the malamute loves to fight just as a healthy small boy loves to play. He will fight his brother or his best friend. So when these dogs piled into Swift Lightning's fight the character of the whole performance was changed. They had no way of knowing that a legitimate quarry was at the bottom of the heap. The first malamute sank his teeth into the neck of an Airedale; a second leaped in, and then a third; and inside of thirty seconds every dog was fighting every other dog irrespective of sex or breed.

Amid this pandemonium of sound Swift Lightning heard indistinctly the voice of a man. It was Bronson, yelling lustily, and swinging his spear. Other figures were running from the ship, and when Swift Lightning rolled at last to the edge of the fight half a dozen Eskimo whips were cutting like knives into the mass of bodies. The tip of one of these whips caught him on the end of his nose as he darted out. A second uncoiled over his back and wrapped itself around his body as he dodged between two figures and ran into the night.

For some time he heard the wild voices of the men and the lashing of their whips. But when he came to the cairn and squatted in his wallow, facing the sea, there was no longer the tumult of battle but a deep silence.

In that silence he sat and waited. He was neither whipped nor afraid of the odds he had fought, yet in him was no longer the desire to wreak vengeance on the creatures of the ship. His dream was broken, and the hope that had lured him to it was gone. Two or three times he circled round the cairn, smelling of the old wallows and the footprints. Then he traveled south.

When he stopped again it was where Firefly had turned from their wanderings in the direction of the ship. It was half chance and half yearning for her that brought him to the sheltered hollow where the storm had not quite covered her footprints. He whimpered as he smelled them and his heart throbbed with a last hope—the hope of the beast that does not reason. Yet he had passed beyond the temptation to go back; the South was calling him now.

He climbed up over the breast of the slope and waited once more. As he looked a living thing came to the edge of the farther rim of the cup and stood profiled against the white mist of the sky. Swift Lightning did not move, but stood like a thing turned suddenly into ice while the creature that was on his trail went down into the hollow and then came up toward him. For he knew that it was not a fox, or a wolf, or one of the fighting dogs from the ship—but Firefly, his mate.

The moon and the stars shone on her as she came. They lit up the questioning eagerness in her eyes and gave to her slim, beautiful body a shimmering golden glow. Yet when she stood at Swift Lightning's side, her silken muzzle against his shaggy shoulder, she was not excited or apologetic, but just warmly and quiveringly glad. Perhaps if she had talked she might have told him that she had had a long sleep, and the fight on the ice had awakened her, and that she was ready now to go wherever he went. And there was a tremulous sound in Swift Lightning's throat.

After a little he turned south—straight south. And Firefly, no longer hesitating, trotted at his side.

CHAPTER XIII

BITTER days were at hand—days when the strongest hunters kept within their habitations and whispered among themselves, *"Neswa ku che wuk* —the three are frozen together," meaning the earth, the sky, and the air. For in that air was a thing more terrifying and as deadly as the most treacherous poison. A thermometer perhaps would not have registered the danger, for men do not necessarily die in a temperature of forty or fifty degrees below zero, and thermometers do not register the unbelievable phenomena of arctic cold. The air was dust dry, and so still that were one venturesome enough to wet a finger and expose it to that air it would freeze simultaneously and evenly on all sides.

It was the stillness that gave warning to all human things. To the ears miles became suddenly so many hundreds of yards. The step of a caribou in the snow-crust could be heard a mile away, a man's cough an equal distance. The horizon seemed to shut in a vast whispering dome. One could have heard voices in ordinary conversation a quarter of a mile away. The sound of a rifle-shot would have carried ten miles.

It was the waning of the long months of polar night

in the great tundras just south of the edge of the Arctic Sea. Night, and yet not night. There was no sun or daylight. The earth had still a few more billion miles to whirl on its axis before the fixed sun would send its first rays over the horizon of the frozen land. But there were stars and a moon and one could have read print under their glow.

In that glow, however, no human being could live. The cracks in the tunnel doors of Eskimo igloos were stuffed tight. Inside the dome-shaped homes of snow and ice burned tiny fires of moss and seal-oil, and people ate—if they had flesh to eat—and waited, and made curious offerings and prayers to heathen gods that missing ones might come back safely. For there were many missing. The terrific cold had come suddenly and swiftly. Many hunters were caught in it. These hunters dug themselves pits in the snow. Out on the sea they made tiny caverns of broken ice, shutting out all air, and buried themselves alive to save their lungs. For it was the lungs that gave out first, and the oldest hunter did not know that he was "touched" until he was dying. Painless and terrible was the sting of this cold, painless because at first it was not felt, terrible because a little later the lungs would slough away in blood.

In this "death cold" beasts still lived and traveled, for nature had given to them what man did not possess. The sparrow does not die in the coldest winter night, because the sparrow's heart beats three times where a man's beats twice; and the blood of a swallow, soaring a thousand yards above the earth, is so hot that in the veins of a human being it would mean death. Caribou and the musk-ox, the fox and the wolf, the big owls and the huge white hares still wandered and sought prey and provender without dread of the cold, for their lungs were protected in two ways. The blood of the arctic fox and the wolf was six degrees hotter than that of the Eskimo, who feared to breathe the outside air, and the blood of the owls was two degrees warmer than the blood of the foxes and the wolves. In the veins of the caribou and the musk-ox there was a temperature of a hundred and two, while in the humans of the Eskimo igloos it was but ninety-eight and three-fifths. For the larger creatures there was still a greater protection. The heat radiation of their nostrils was enormous. They breathed deeply and freely of the oxygen that would have killed a man, but the air was warmed before it reached their lungs.

In this cold traveled Swift Lightning and Firefly—straight into the heart of the vast shrubless and tree-less barrens that lay between the broken tundras of the arctic coast and the first timber-land hundreds of miles south. They had come fifty miles, and in Firefly's slender body was growing a great exhaustion. In Swift Lightning, in place of exhaustion there was an increasing exaltation, a growing pride and joy in the knowledge of his possessorship. His magnificent body was untouched by fatigue. Behind him he was leaving nothing that he yearned for. He no longer wanted to run with the wolves, or lead the great pack. That he had been greatest of all the wolves gave him no thrill now.

He was like a creature that had at last found a way of escaping from an unpleasant thing, and had it not been for Firefly he would have gone on steadily. He would have covered a hundred miles where they had traveled but fifty. He would have run until his sides were gaunt and his eyes were red. But Firefly held him back. Her lowest whimper was sufficient to bring him to her, with an answering whine in his throat. Her tender feet, unaccustomed to rough ice and snow, had begun to bleed early in their journey, and whenever they stopped Swift Lightning licked them with his warm tongue and muzzled her yellow body as Firefly herself had often caressed the white hand of her mistress, a thousand miles away.

Several hours ago they had left the last of the broken tundra, and they were now in the heart of a vast gray chaos of barren, weirdly illuminated from the skies. As they trotted, there rose from their heated bodies a thin, vaporish mist of steam, and this phenomenon of intense arctic cold trailed out behind them like a ghostly streamer for a quarter of a mile. A band of running caribou would have left that same ghostly trail in the air five times the distance behind their galloping hoofs. Their scent drifted even farther from their bodies. It hung low and heavy and strong in the air. In the days of the great cold the odor of a caribou herd is like a stench in a man's nostrils at a distance of two miles, where in ordinary weather it cannot be smelled more than three or four hundred yards. And it was this smell, the effluvium rising from a herd of caribou, that came suddenly to the nostrils of Swift Lightning and Firefly.

In a flash Swift Lightning had stopped, and was pointing the direction of the scent. To Firefly it meant little. She was hungry. It was fifteen hours ago that she had eaten last of the flesh of a hare which Swift Lightning had killed. But the scent that was now in the air did not thrill her with the promise of food. It was like the bodily exhalation of a cow or a horse, and she was acquainted with both. They had never meant food to her. But in Swift Lightning there was a tense and eager excitement. He turned from their southward direction and struck west. If there was the faintest movement in the air it was from that direction.

Firefly followed him, swiftly sensing the fact that in the scent was some mysterious thing which thrilled her mate. The caribou were two or three thousand yards to the west, behind a low ridge that rose out of the breast of the barren. Had it been day, one could have seen over the top of that ridge a white, vaporish

mist—the phenomenon of steam rising from the bodies
of the animals on the other side. Very soon the sharp
ears of both Swift Lightning and Firefly caught sound,
even at that distance of three-quarters of a mile or
so. Standing still, they heard plainly the caribou's
antlers as they ripped up the frozen snow in quest of
the crisp green moss underneath, and the tramp of
their hoofs was as if they were but a rifle-shot away.

Because of their apparent nearness Swift Lightning
moved slowly and with great caution. It was half an
hour before he made the foot of the low ridge. Up
this he climbed, with Firefly close at his heels. At the
crest he flattened himself out on his belly, and Firefly, learning swiftly of her mate, did likewise.

Below them were the caribou. There were probably
fifty or sixty within their vision, chiefly females and
under-yearlings. One of these young females was
almost directly under Swift Lightning, and his eyes
measured the space between. The next instant he was
at his prey. So sudden was the attack that Firefly
was left paralyzed with astonishment. Under the vivid
glow of the moon and the stars she looked down on an
amazing thing. She had seen Swift Lightning fight
Wapusk, the polar bear, but it had been a defensive
fight. Now she saw him for the first time in the might
of his prowess. He was at the throat of a creature
three times as large as himself, and together they went
down.

Her blood ran with fear as she heard the sudden thunder of a hundred hoofs; but the great dark forms of the caribou did not attack; they were running away. She raised her head. Below her Swift Lightning and the under-yearling twisted and rolled, and fought on the hoof-torn snow. Her blood raced with a sudden thrill. Swift Lightning's snarling came to her, and her lips bared until they showed her milk-white teeth, and into her eyes came a strange fire. Then she shot down the slope.

But she was too late to be of assistance to Swift Lightning. The under-yearling was almost dead. In a few moments the struggle ceased, and Swift Lightning stood up. Firefly's bright eyes were on him. In that hour she was filled with the great pride of one who has sent her mate forth to battle, and welcomes him back again a victor. For a moment or two she stood with her silken muzzle against his shoulder. And then Swift Lightning ripped open the young caribou.

Together they feasted. After that Firefly lay down beside the warm carcass and dropped into a sleep of exhaustion.

After a time Swift Lightning dozed at her side. It was an hour later when he got up and nibbled at the flesh of the young caribou. It was frozen solid as a rock. He roused Firefly with a whine and she rose stiffly to her feet. In her body was a strange numbness. Under her jaw her breath had formed a chunk of ice which she proceeded to scrape off with her forepaws.

Swift Lightning led the way. Instinct told him they had slept to the last minute in that terrific cold. The treacherous grip of it was in his body. Attempting to trot, Firefly felt unwieldy and cumbersome. It was colder, if possible, than a few hours before. The air from their lungs transformed itself into white frost the instant it left their mouths. For a time their stiffened bodies, chilled by the inactivity of their rest, did not leave the ghostly trails in the air behind them. But they grew swiftly warmer. Their blood ran faster. The stiffness left their legs and bodies, and in a quarter of an hour they were trotting steadily southward.

Though Firefly was fresher because of food and rest, Swift Lightning did not quicken his pace. He did not reason. He did not work out mentally the finer problems of life and death, yet a hand was guiding him—the hand of a superhuman instinct. It told him not only which direction was south—dead south; it told him also not to run fast, as it was his joy to run at times, but to trot steadily. For to have run until he panted through open jaws, or until he broke into sweat, would have meant giving himself up at last to the teeth of the deadly cold.

Hour after hour they went on, and many times in those hours they stopped and rested. Three times Firefly flopped down on the snow, but each time Swift

Lightning stood erect on his feet, and after a certain time had passed urged her to follow him on. It was forty hours after they had left the edge of the sea before the cold began to break. In two hours the temperature rose twenty degrees. Not until then did Swift Lightning let Firefly stop for the long rest she wanted. In the shelter of a snow-dune they made their wallows, and for many hours after that they slept.

Neither Swift Lightning nor Firefly noticed the slow but steady change that was taking place in their world when they went on again. The stars seemed to be receding and growing smaller, and they no longer blazed but burned dully. The mystic illumination in the heart of the sky was steadily fading away; their vision was not so clear, and they could not see so far. For Swift Lightning and Firefly were entering into the edge of that weird and mysterious "world between" —that strip around the neck of the earth where the long arctic night dissolves into the day of the far northern sun. Each hour added to the change, as one by one the stars faded out and disappeared.

Twice again they slept, and then there came a period when there were no stars at all in the heaven above them, and the world was a great gray chaos of twilight. Another day and another night, and Swift Lightning and Firefly woke from their fourth sleep to face the great phenomenon. Over the southern bulge of the earth the sun was peeping.

It was only a glow—a pale crimson splash as if a great fire was brightening a patch of the sky from behind a hill many miles away. Trembling, their hearts thumping excitedly in their bodies, Swift Lightning and Firefly stared at it. They *knew*. And in these precious and wonderful moments they did not move.

The crimson grew more vivid, and then, as suddenly as it had come, it faded away and was gone. For perhaps ten minutes that glow had pointed the sky, and in the hearts of Swift Lightning and Firefly there remained a great thrill. They forgot their exhaustion and their sore feet and their hunger. *They had seen the sun!* For the first time in many months they had seen it, and their souls cried out in all the gladness of the blind who suddenly see the dawning of light. It was their first day—a day of only ten minutes in length, following a night of twenty-three hours and fifty minutes.

Toward that point where the sun had disappeared they trotted swiftly and steadily. Firefly herself killed a big white rabbit. A little later Swift Lightning killed another. They devoured this meat, but they did not stop to lie down and sleep. Through many hours of night they traveled—night that was not like the night up on the edge of the frozen sea. For the moon was farther away, and much of the time hidden behind clouds. At the end of thirty miles sheer exhaustion made Firefly curl herself up in the snow. It was not

very cold now. The temperature was not more than
eight or ten below zero. And for the fifth time they
slept.

It was Swift Lightning's howl that roused Firefly—a howl that came out of his throat as never another
howl had come before; and Firefly opened her eyes
and raised her head, and found the sun shining in her
face. It was the sun this time. There was no heat
to it, unless it was the heat fired in the blood of living
things by the mere sight of its flaming glory. It was
like a great ball of dull fire, a monster ball. Neither
Swift Lightning nor Firefly had ever seen a sun so
large. It did not quite lift itself entirely above the
bulge of the earth's surface, but for close to half an
hour a part of it was visible; and even after the ball
itself was gone the glow remained in the sky, so that
this day was an hour and thirty minutes in length.

And now there came another change. The barren
was no longer what it had been fifty miles nearer to
the coast. Here and there were small patches of
stunted timber growth. The junipers and larches of
the tundras gave way to the first of the black and
white spruce, and these were soon intermingled with
aspen and Bank's pine and clumps of birch and balsam.
The next time Swift Lightning and Firefly stopped to
rest and sleep they made their wallows in the shelter
of a dense little evergreen thicket. After this each
night grew shorter and each day grew longer; and the

scrub thickets grew into what is called *misti-koos*, or
stunted timber; and the stunted timber grew steadily
larger—until at last Swift Lightning knew that he
was in another world than any he had ever known before, and that a part of his dream had come true.

When they struck the forest country it was Firefly
who gave him courage and confidence in his new environment. All his life a creature of the open barrens,
with neither forest nor swamp to break their illimitable monotony, these things amazed him now, and filled
him with wonder. To Firefly they were the intimate
things of home. They came suddenly upon their first
moose, a huge bull with massive antlers five feet from
tip to tip, and as they faced this monster scarcely
twenty feet from them Firefly was no less appalled than
Swift Lightning. The musk-ox, with its battlemented
head, he would have attacked, but Mooswa, the old
bull, held him back; and for the first time in his life
Swift Lightning circled round a creature with hoofs.

They traveled slowly now, for to Swift Lightning
there was no longer a lure far ahead. Days added
themselves into weeks. They came into the larger
timber country, crossed rivers and lakes, and left their
trail through the hearts of great swamps. The joy of
a new life entered into Swift Lightning. There was
food, more food than he had ever known in all his
life. The swamps were filled with it. In one great
swamp they lived for ten days. The snow was beaten

hard with the tracks of rabbits. It was *wapoos oo skow*—the "big year" of the rabbits—in these regions, and there were thousands, and tens of thousands, and hundreds of thousands of them. In places their padded feet had beaten the snow until it was hard as ice. At night, under the glow of the stars, they could hear the *thump, thump, thump* of rabbit feet, like a dull and steady tattoo on the earth, so many were they. Hunting them ceased to have a thrill. And as the sun climbed higher in the heaven each day Swift Lightning and Firefly grew steadily fatter in their paradise.

Even Firefly had little desire now to leave this new world into which they had come. Her one desire was to keep at Swift Lightning's side; and once, when by chance she had wandered away, Swift Lightning let out a howl of wild anxiety that echoed far and wide through the forest. Three times they came on the cabins of men, and a dozen times they struck trails made by snowshoes and moccasins. Twice Firefly showed a desire to go to the cabins, but Swift Lightning held her back. The third time, sensing from his caution that there was something about them to evade, she did not hesitate to follow when he led quickly back into the thickness of the timber.

And then came spring.

By that time Firefly herself was a creature of the wilderness. Her golden coat was longer and shaggier. Many times her milk-white teeth had killed for food, and in her blood ran now the age-old thrill of the chase. In the three months of her matehood with Swift Lightning she had lived three years. The master who was dead was not forgotten, but it seemed a very long time ago that he had lived. Swift Lightning filled her life and her world. Yet her dreams came to her vividly at times, dreams of the man, and of the woman, and of other things she had known. In those dreams she would whimper, and it was then that Swift Lightning would muzzle her closely, as if he understood.

CHAPTER XIV

WEEKS later, in the days just before the flood rains, Swift Lightning and Firefly found themselves in a verdant wilderness just south and west of Great Slave Lake in the almost unknown country between the River du Rocher and the unnamed stream that empties into it from the east. They were three hundred miles south of the barren lands, and the fulness of spring had come. Up the unnamed stream, which the government itself had mapped only by dotted lines, they found splendid hunting. It was a beautiful country, filled with great ridges, deep gullies, lakes and rivers, and wonderful forests. Sometimes the ridges were so high they were almost like small mountains, and between them were mysterious valleys out of which ran hundreds of little streams, all emptying into the unnamed river that ran to the west.

Never had Swift Lightning seen grass so green and soft and so thick under his feet, and never had he smelled so many sweet things in the air. For the whole earth was bursting with the life and joy of spring. The spruce and cedar and balsam were taking on a new sheen. The first of the early flowers were out. The poplar buds had grown overfat and burst into tender leaf. Everywhere was the hum and the smell and the gladness of new life.

On the green slopes of the ridges, where the sun had struck first, the black bears and their cubs came to feed. In the meadows between wandered moose and caribou. The lakes were alive with wild fowl, and the mating-songs of birds rose up from the fens and thickets. And with all this there was a droning, musical sound in the air—a sound that seemed always of the same volume night and day—the rippling music of water running down between the ridges and in the valleys.

Swift Lightning and Firefly loved to hunt along the unnamed river. It was one of those occasional streams of the Northland with a very wide channel and thousands of sand-bars. It was wild and picturesque, and gave great promise to the hunter. Its two shores were shelving, like the shores of a lake, and were of sand and pebbles and boulders. These wide, flat shores and the innumerable sand-bars had caught the driftage of many years—driftage that was bleached white as chalk and in many places ten or fifteen feet high. It was a shallow stream before the floods, so that more than once Swift Lightning and Firefly crossed it by wading or swimming through water from sand-bar to sand-bar. The great piles of bleached driftage held a fascination for them, and they loved to climb over them and explore their mysteries.

At a point where the river rambled out over a shallow bed an eighth of a mile wide lay Kwahoo, the great drift. For a decade the occasional Indian hunters who had wandered up and down had called it by that name. It lay anchored to a sand-bar in the middl of the river bed, and for many years had defied the rush of floods. It was a hundred feet long by twice as wide, and it had the appearance of having been built by an army of mighty carpenters especially to mock at the force of the waters. Hundreds of tree trunks had jammed and interlaced themselves into its making, and they were as white as the desert-bleached bones of a skeleton.

One early evening in the crimson light of a setting sun Swift Lightning and Firefly made their way to it. The water in the broad part of the stream was very shallow, and they hardly wet their shoulders on the way. The top of the drift, which was five or six feet above the level of the water, was even more attractive than the part of it which they had seen from the shore. So closely jammed were the smooth white logs that they were like a floor, and all that day they had been absorbing the warmth of the sun. At one end a number of logs had forced themselves upward by driving their butts into the river-bed below, and had formed as nice a shelter for two as Swift Lightning and Firefly had ever found.

Until dark they wandered over the white floor of

Kwahoo. This evening the sun went out suddenly. Scarcely was it gone when there came from the far west the low grumbling of thunder, and very soon after that the far-away flash of lightning. Swift Lightning sniffed the air and sensed the coming of the storm. At the first rumble of thunder Firefly buried herself in the far end of the shelter on the top of Kwahoo. She had always been afraid of thunder and lightning, and half a dozen times Swift Lightning ran back to her from the edge of the drift, urging her to come ashore with him. In the growing darkness her eyes glowed steadily but she did not move. And at last Swift Lightning came in and flattened himself down beside her, with a whine of anxiety in his throat. Firefly in response drew a deep breath of relief and rested her muzzle on his shoulder.

The storm descended swiftly on the forest world. It swept over Kwahoo in a lightning-flamed deluge; and as Firefly saw the ghostly bones of the drift in the vivid flare she crept still closer to her protector and hid her head behind him.

Up the river went the storm. The thousand little trickles among the ridges became suddenly so many racing rivulets, swelling the tiny watercourses in the coulées; the water from these coulées flooded the channels of little streams, and these streams rushed boisterously into larger creeks, and the larger creeks emptied into the unnamed river. For an hour the deluge fell, and then it quieted down to a steady, pouring rain. All night it kept up, and with morning it was still raining. It was not a hard rain, but monotonously steady, and the sky was gray and thick.

Swift Lightning and Firefly went out early into the drizzle and over the slippery floor of Kwahoo to the river. It was not the gentle rippling sound of the day before that filled their ears now, but the swift and menacing rush of swelling waters. The warm yellow sand-bars over which they traveled yesterday had disappeared. Between them and the shore was a roaring torrent. On all sides of Kwahoo it was the same. They were caught in the beginning of the flood-water, and the drift alone was their refuge.

With each hour after that the river rose swiftly and steadily. Twice again that morning the rain fell in torrents, and by mid-afternoon the flood had risen within two feet of the top of the drift. The roar of it was deafening. In its mighty rush Kwahoo rocked and trembled, but its deep and mysterious anchorage held it, as it had held it for many years past. Awed and yet unafraid, Swift Lightning and Firefly watched the terrific spectacle. The forests and swamps and sand-bars were giving up their driftage, and a monster and varied procession of it swept by. Now and then a mass would strike Kwahoo, and the giant drift would shudder at the blow; but always it stood fast, battering the smaller driftage out into the stream.

Darkness and night came again, and through the black hours it rained steadily. The tumult of the deluge increased. Its roaring grew deeper, and not once did Swift Lightning and Firefly close their eyes. From their shelter they stared out into the chaos of storm and waited for light again. It came at last, and they went out on what was left of Kwahoo. Parts of it had been torn away, but still the massive heart of the drift was left, a hundred feet square.

At its upper end the flood had thrown a fresh pile of débris, and Firefly and Swift Lightning advanced to investigate it. For nearly forty hours they had not eaten, and hunger pressed them. In the edge of the driftage a furry, diamond-eyed creature lay flat on its belly, watching them from between its forepaws. A dozen times since coming into the forests Swift Lightning had seen lynxes, but never one as large as the huge cat that had been thrown upon Kwahoo. There was something about Pisew, the lynx, that spoke also of hunger. He had gone even longer than they without food. Swift Lightning half circled him cautiously. A menacing growl was in his throat, to which the lynx made no answer except that his nose crinkled, his lips drew up a bit, and his whiskers bristled. Firefly whimpered and ran after her mate, urging him back.

And then, so swiftly that none of them moved during its occurrence, an amazing thing happened.

Down the breast of that rolling, thunderous flood

came the frailest of all the things that had beaten against the drift—a birch-bark canoe. In it were a man and a woman, and clutched tightly in the woman's arms a child. The woman's face was dead white, whiter because of the thick masses of shining black hair that fell loosely about her, clinging wet about her face and shoulders and body. And, if his beard had not hidden it, Gaston Rouget's face would have shone as bloodless as the woman's. For he had seen death ahead of them in each minute of the last half-hour—ever since they had been driven from their flood-destroyed cabin to make a fight for their lives in the canoe. Vainly he had fought to reach the shore, but all he could do was keep the nose of his canoe straight ahead.

And now, dead in his way, lay the drift.

"Jeanne, *ma chérie,* there is nothing to fear now!" he cried bravely to the woman ahead of him. "There is Kwahoo, and the water is sweeping over the end of it. I shall run straight on. Hold tight to little Jeanne."

The canoe rushed up over the submerged end of Kwahoo. It struck and flopped sideways, and the woman was flung out, still clutching the little girl. Gaston Rouget scrambled to them like a many-legged and many-armed man, and caught them madly to his breast while the canoe, lightened of its human burden, swung out into the flood with their food, Rouget's rifle, and the blankets.

Gaston, seeing it go, held his loved ones still closer while a new horror struck to his heart. From their refuge, in that moment, he saw no way of escape for many days, and with the canoe had also gone the bread and meat that would have given them life. Then, rising to his feet, he saw the great cat crouching on an upthrown log, and beyond it, standing out clear on the flood-wood, the alert and poised forms of Firefly and Swift Lightning. Instinctively his hand reached to the one weapon he possessed now—the knife at his belt, and the cold chill went out of his heart; for in these three he saw what he had given up as lost— food and life for many days.

"Le bon Dieu be praised!" he said, speaking to the woman, yet with his huntsman's eyes on the cat and the dog and the wolf. "It is fortunate that we were thrown upon Kwahoo, my Jeanne—it is fortunate!"

CHAPTER XV

FOR Swift Lightning and Firefly the whimsical twistings of a few minutes had changed a thrilling adventure into a still greater thrill of impending tragedy. In their discovery of the lynx they had sensed instantly the presence of a deadly enemy; and the big cat, eyeing them from his log, trembled with the thrill of a great desire. That desire was to get at the throat of the dog.

At the bottom of the instincts of all was hunger. It was greatest in the lank-bellied, famished cat. In Swift Lightning its demand had not yet told him that Pisew was meat to kill and devour, yet it was the fearlessness and the unformed desire of hunger that held him in his tracks when Firefly tried to urge him back. He was ready to give battle to anything of flesh and blood—except man; and Pisew, crouching on his log, waited for the distance to shorten between them so that he might leap. In that wait had come a man.

The presence of that most dominant animal of all creation drove another thing than the fire of desire and hate through their veins. It was fear—the fear of the ages. Pisew cringed flatter that he might not be seen, and Swift Lightning dropped back snarling, his ears flattened. Only Firefly did not move. Her bright eyes were filled with wonderment at the appearance of the man and the woman and of the little child who stood between them, clutching at the woman's hand.

It was at Firefly that Gaston Rouget stared in amazement. Never had wolf given birth to a creature like her. He whispered it to the woman while his fingers gripped tighter the handle of his knife. A dog! He called and advanced a few steps, holding out his hand. He called to her in Cree, and in French, and in English. He was within ten paces of her when she turned and trotted back to Swift Lightning.

It was he who urged upon her a mysterious sense of danger. She stood close to him, conscious of the quivering snarl in his throat. Yet in that moment she wanted to go to the man, and especially to the woman and the child.

The man understood. In his face was a new light of gladness. He worshiped the woman with the long shining hair and his soul was wrapped up in the little Jeanne. They had faced death—now he saw life. In his pockets were matches. There was dry wood to be had by digging into the white logs under his feet, and in his belt was a knife. He foresaw that the yellow dog which had wandered away with a wolf would be easy to lure and easy to kill. They would not starve on Kwahoo.

In the steady, drizzling downpour of the rain the

man went toward the middle of the dead-wood raft, holding the woman by the hand. The water ran in little trickles from her long black hair, and little Jeanne's lighter hair was plastered wet round her face and shoulders. The man came first to the upheaved logs which had formed the dry nest occupied by Swift Lightning and Firefly, and when he looked in he gave an exclamation of joy.

From a little distance Firefly and her mate watched the interlopers. They saw them enter their cavern of logs, and Swift Lightning's snarl was filled with a sullen rage. Inside the man stripped off the child's wet clothes while the woman twisted her heavy hair and wrung the water from it. Then she leaned over and put her arms around both the man and the child and kissed the man. Gaston Rouget laughed softly and a little later began digging up dry splinters of spruce with his knife. Soon after that Swift Lightning and Firefly saw a thin veil of gray smoke rising out of their stolen kennel, and Pisew smelled the tang of it in the sodden air.

All that day Kwahoo shuddered and shivered in the mighty force of the flood, but the anchorage under it held fast. Again and again the man came out of his shelter and approached as close as he could to Firefly. Three times the woman came with him, and once Firefly let her come very near. In her voice there was no lure of death for Gaston had not told her what was in his mind. Her eyes glowed softly. Her voice was gentle. In the reach of her arms was the desire to fondle, the desire to make friends. Yet Firefly remained always just out of reach, warned by Swift Lightning's snarling voice.

Night came again. It was thick and black, but the rain had ceased. Pisew crept out of his drift-pile, and his claws tensed hungrily into the wood under his padded feet. Swift Lightning, with eyes of fire, watched and waited and sniffed the air cautiously and expectantly. In the shelter of logs only the woman and the child slept. The man was wide awake, his hand resting always on a club he had found. In her sleep little Jeanne murmured sobbingly. Gaston understood. It was hunger. He put out his head and listened. The rush of the flood smothered other sound, but he heard something that was like the ripping of claws in wood and as he caught the flash of a pair of greenish eyes his hand gripped the club at his side.

In the early hours of morning, black as the midnight, Firefly approached the shelter of logs. The man heard the sound of her claws ten feet away and he laid his club aside and drew out his knife. Nearer and still nearer came Firefly—and ten steps behind her was Swift Lightning. To Gaston the minutes were hours before Firefly came to the opening. She thrust in her head and he heard her sniffing. Then came her shoulders and even in the blackness he knew that she was half in. From the side he reached out one hand an inch at a time, and in his other he raised the knife. Then, swift as Pisew himself, he lunged out and his fingers gripped in Firefly's yellow hair. The knife drove through the pit of darkness. It struck flesh and bone, and Firefly's howl of agony was followed by the clashing of Swift Lightning's fangs as he rushed in. The woman woke with a scream, and Gaston struck out blindly twice more. But Firefly was gone, leaving a handful of her yellow hair in his fingers. The knife had struck her shoulder-blade, ripping down through the flesh, and a stream of blood dripped from her wound as she ran with Swift Lightning for the far end of Kwahoo.

A few minutes afterward Pisew came upon the warm red trail and his big body twitched. Foot by foot he stalked over it through the darkness, until at last coming round the end of the drift-pile he met the blazing eyes of Swift Lightning. It was the leader of the packs who leaped first.

Gaston Rouget, searching for the dog that he hoped he had wounded to death, heard the tumult of battle above the roar of flood. Greater hope filled his heart. The dog had dragged herself away, and the wolf and the lynx were fighting over her, he thought. Holding his club he approached the sound of combat cautiously. When he came to the rolling and twisting bodies he struck twice in the darkness. Pisew's night-eyes saw him first, and the lynx leaped up and over the drift. A third blow touched Swift Lightning's shoulder and he, too, was gone. On his hands and knees, Gaston Rouget searched. His fingers touched warm blood. But Firefly was not there, dead of her wound, as he had hoped. She was with Swift Lightning at the lower end of the big drift.

The man went back to the shelter where Jeanne and the little Jeanne were waiting, frightened. Pisew moved again out of his flood-wood lair and smelled hungrily of the blood stains left by Firefly. Swift Lightning, his sides ripped by the cat's long claws, shifted his wide-open eyes like search-lights. A thing mightier in its instinct than hunger was in his blood. It was the passionate desire of the beast to defend his mate. Firefly was whimpering softly with pain. He muzzled her gently, yet his body was hard as steel. A dozen times he caught the flash of Pisew's eyes out on the white logs of Kwahoo before dawn came.

This day it was lighter. Gaston Rouget knew that the rains had passed but that the flood would boil for many days. His heart sank when he saw that Firefly was alive and limping but slightly.

Even the woman could not approach near to her now. Hardly a step did she move away from Swift Lightning's shoulder.

In the older Jeanne's dark eyes was a growing terror, and more frequently little Jeanne cried and asked for something to eat. Gaston put his arms around them both and laughed cheerfully to keep up their courage. All that day he stalked with his club. In the afternoon an inspiration came to him when he saw the three or four places where Pisew entered and came out of his drift-pile. With new hope the woman unbraided her long hair when Gaston told her his plan. Each shining strand was precious to him, yet from it he cut enough to make three snares stronger than rope or wire. And just before the dusk of another night he set these for the lynx.

Again he waited after darkness came, with his club close at hand. Softly the woman crooned little Jeanne to restless sleep. This night she did not close her eyes, but sat with her head resting against Gaston's shoulder and in her heart prayed for the thing to happen which he had promised her.

Pisew had lived many years and had encountered many perils. He knew the smell of man and the menace of man, and when in the blackness of the night he came to the first of the silken snares the perfume of it stopped him dead in his tracks. To him it bore the taint of poison. He avoided it and wormed himself a new way out of the tangled drift.

His craving tonight was no longer mere hunger; it was a madness. His padded feet moved silently over the logs until he found the quarter of wind that brought with it the scent of Firefly. For half an hour he lay flat. Then a foot at a time he began to stalk his prey. Starvation gave him terrible courage. He was not afraid of Swift Lightning, nor would he have been afraid of two or three Swift Lightnings. With his long claws he had killed caribou and in his second year he had slain a wolf.

Swift Lightning caught no scent because the wind was against him, but after a time he saw the greenish flashings of Pisew's eyes as he came nearer and nearer through the darkness.

He made no effort to avoid the climax of what he sensed to be a great tragedy. Firefly's fear as she, too, saw the advancing eyes added to the determination that was in his brain. He did not stir, but as the gleaming eyes advanced Firefly crawled back a bit at a time. From the door of their shelter Gaston and Jeanne stared out into the pit of darkness, waiting, listening, watchful. They, too, had seen the flash of eyes, and in a whisper the man explained what was about to happen and what it would mean for them. For it would be a fight to the death, and after that there would be meat to last them until the flood went down.

Their blood ran swift and hot as they heard the first clash of the mighty duel that was fought in the blackness of Kwahoo that night. The woman covered the ears of little Jeanne so that she would not be awakened to the horror of it. Not even Firefly's eyes could see what was happening in the first moments of the combat. Swift Lightning had shot like a rocket for the big cat when he was ten feet distant, and Pisew had hardly time to throw himself on his back in the terrible and deadly fighting position of the lynx when the wolf-dog's jaws were at his throat.

For perhaps two or three minutes the unseen combat continued; and then suddenly the fear swept out of Firefly's heart, and into her veins shot the fire of the fighting collie. It was Swift Lightning, her mate, who was fighting and he was fighting for her. She sensed that. It gripped her, and like a little demon she leaped into the struggle. Her teeth were sharper than Swift Lightning's though not so long and in her first enraged lunge they pierced the cat's loin. They sank deep and tore viciously. Again and again they ripped; and in that hour, just as Swift Lightning had saved her from Wapusk, the bear, so did Firefly save him from the lynx. For in the darkness Swift Lightning was fighting an enemy who was strange to him, and whose tricks of combat he had not learned. Torn and bleeding as he was, he was given a chance by Firefly's attack for his neck-hold, and in another two minutes Pisew was dead.

Through the darkness the man was coming with his club, and Swift Lightning and Firefly left the body of their slain enemy and stole to the upper end of Kwahoo, where for a long time Firefly gently nursed the wounds of her mate with her soft red tongue.

When day came the woman with the shining hair came near and tossed them chunks of raw meat which only Firefly touched; and the man, crossing himself devoutly, swore that no matter what chance came to him he would not harm these beasts that had given them life on Kwahoo, for surely they had been placed there by *le bon Dieu*, their Master.

The second day thereafter Swift Lightning ate of the meat that had on it the taint of human hands; and for three more days the flesh of the lynx was divided evenly between man and beast. On the seventh day Firefly and Swift Lightning swam ashore, and the man and the woman watched them go. Gaston whispered that tomorrow they also would go, while in the woman's dark eyes there was a soft glow—and tears.

CHAPTER XVI

TRESOR was a one-man dog, and Tresor's master was a one-dog man. Gaston Rouget was that master, and Jeanne, with the long, black, shining hair, was his mistress, and the baby Jeanne, in her fourth glorious summer of life, was the divinity at whose little feet he worshiped. After the great spring flood there was a period of sorrow as well as rejoicing in the new cabin of logs which Gaston built in the great wilderness country just east of Great Slave Lake. For Tresor could not be taken in the canoe when they escaped from their inundated home, and they believed he must have died in the flood. But he had not given up the ghost so easily, and the new cabin was hardly more than built when he heard the ring of his master's ax one day, and came to them, hungry and glad.

Tresor was a giant and the blood in him was mostly mastiff. Five years ago, early in the winter, Gaston and Jeanne had left a plague-stricken country for new trapping-grounds farther north, and it was Tresor who had pulled their sledge and all their belongings. Through dark days and clear, when hopes were high and hopes were low in the hearts of Jeanne and Gaston, Tresor's splendid body never for an instant failed, and like a loyal slave he made it possible for them to reach their journey's end on the River du Rocher. And there, in the glory of their first spring, the little Jeanne was born.

It was because he was a one-man dog and a one-woman dog and a one-baby dog that Tresor was not like other dogs of the forest country. A savage world had not made him cruel. He killed, but it was not for the love of killing. And he did not run with the wolves or go away in the mating-season, which was a miracle to Gaston Rouget. It was in these days that a deep and oppressing loneliness pressed upon Tresor, and his soul was filled with the yearning for a mate and the joys of matehood.

And Gaston would caress his head and say in the soft and picturesque English which he used when he did not speak in French:

"You Montrea-al dog, Tresor, an' Montrea-al is dam' long way off! You dreaming about Montrea-al she-dog, an' he never come. *Tonnere!* Why you no listen to ze wolf? He howl. He call. He ask you come an' mate an' have ze babies—an' I tell you Montrea-al dam' far off, an' you better go an' come back lak good dog. You go. I say good-by an' you come back, Tresor. All ze wil' dog do that. When there is no dog then she take ze wolf."

And Gaston would slap Tresor on the shoulder as he would have slapped a man, grinning as he thought of what his dark-haired Jeanne would say if she could hear his monstrous advice.

But Tresor never went.

"You too dam' much p'tic'lar," Gaston explained to him in confidence, using the biggest word in his English vocabulary for emphasis. "Wolf *iskwao,* she be pretty much beeg fool!"

Then this double-faced Gaston Rouget would say, in a different language, to his lovely wife, "There never was another dog like Tresor, *ma chérie.* Have I not given him great training that, even in the mating-season, he does not leave us for the wolves, or even for Le Duc's scraggly mongrel beasts over beyond the cedar ridges?"

And Jeanne would afterward hug Tresor's big head in her arms and sometimes dream of the forests farther south, where there were cabins and people and friends. For even in the happiness of her possession of Gaston and the little Jeanne there were times when she, too, was lonely.

Then came the night, filled with stars, and a great moon, when Tresor heard drifting to him faintly a sound that he had never before heard in all this wilderness. It was not the cry of a lynx; it was not the scream of a loon; it was not the bellowing of a moose and it was not the howl of wolf or husky. It was the thing of which he had dreamed and for which he had waited—*the barking of a dog!*

More than a mile away, from the crest of a ridge, Firefly was barking at a moose passing through the shimmer of yellow and gold in the plain below her. Close beside her stood Swift Lightning. In all her experience and adventure since she had abandoned ship and men and dogs she had not ceased to bark at other creatures of the wild when she was not hungry, and when she knew there was no necessity for food. To Swift Lightning her barking was a rare and wonderful music. It never failed to thrill him for it was music that went back to the kennels of his forefathers, back through long years to the things which had come to him only in dreams—dreams which were more and more real as weeks and months passed in the deep forest country.

He was no longer the killer of old. From great heights he had fallen, and happiness had come with that fall. Where he had mastered, now he was ruled —except where the grim business of life or death lay before him. Just as a strong man finds himself guided by the little finger of the woman he loves, so Swift Lightning found himself now the slave of Firefly.

It was, after all, a delightful slavery for him. For in the hunt, when hunger pressed them, Firefly soft-footed at his side or just behind him, watching his every movement. And when there was thunder and lightning she would creep close to him and snuggle her head against his neck. And when *she* wanted to sleep she would lie close against him, knowing that in the nearness of him was her protection. But when danger came to Swift Lightning, as in that night when he battled the giant lynx, she forgot both femininity and fear. It was she who had killed Pisew many weeks ago; and it was only today those same milk-white teeth had nipped Swift Lightning's shoulder because he had lured her to a brush-heap where a wood-beetle had grabbed her nose.

Tonight the tiny plateau at the crest of the ridge held Firefly, and Swift Lightning was satisfied. A dozen leaps would have carried him across this plateau. It was a spot not more than fifty or sixty feet square, on which the grass grew thick and luxuriant because of a spring that bubbled straight up through the heart of the ridge. Frequently they had come to this spring, and it was a pleasant place to lie after a hot day.

But until tonight Firefly had not barked from the crest of this ridge. They had never traveled farther down it and they knew nothing of Gaston Rouget's cabin. They had not yet smelled the smoke of it nor had they crossed a man-trail, for Gaston's journeys were short in these days of summer. Their paradise was their own. And though there was not a drop of the wolf-blood in her veins Firefly was happy in this world. She loved to hunt. She loved to run swiftly at the side of her wild-born mate. She loved the cool forests, the deep swamps, the hidden lakes, and the twisting streams. And tonight, even after the bull moose had passed, she continued to bark in the glad thrill of life that possessed her; and because she was his mate and the world was beautiful Swift Lightning's heart beat warm and exultant within him.

Toward the joyous cry came Tresor. It was not the mating-season but that did not lessen the thrill that ran in his blood. A long time he had waited and dreamed, and winter or summer he would have answered the call that came to him on the wind. He plunged through the thick forest. Had his mistress or his master called him then he would have been deaf to the command. When he came to the foot of the big ridge he stopped. Vainly he listened, and in his throat grew a low whine. But Firefly was no longer barking at the moon-filled plain, and Tresor climbed the ridge slowly, sniffing the air for that which he could no longer hear. The path he took was the trail of Kak, the fat porcupine, who came twice each day to drink at the spring which watered the tiny green meadow on the crest of the ridge.

It was Firefly who sensed his coming first. She had gone to the far edge of the little meadow, where the porcupine's trail came up, leaving Swift Lightning stretched out close to the edge of the plateau. The wind was against her, but at the foot of the ridge it eddied in an upward current, and in that reflected air came the scent of Tresor, which Swift Lightning could not catch, but which filled the nostrils of his mate. And in that thrilling instant she knew the difference. It was not the smell of wolf. It was the body-odor of her father, her mother, and of the little brothers and sisters she had romped with long ago.

It set her trembling, just as if she had known that the master who was dead under his cairn of rocks far north was coming up through the haze of the ridge-side.

She did not advance to meet it, nor did she retreat, but lay flat and waited. Swift Lightning, looking lazily off over the plain, did not see what happened then. Tresor, his muscles rigid, came up within ten feet of Firefly. Beyond her he saw nothing, smelled nothing. His eyes blazed in the pale light and Firefly—as if to let him know where she was—stood up again on her feet and still waited. Slowly he advanced. They made no sound but their eyes were like burning coals.

It was Tresor's whine of joy that turned Swift Lightning's head. He saw a great beast standing near Firefly, and he saw Firefly's head muzzling that monster, and then, in a moment that seemed to freeze all life within him, he saw her begin to caper about the interloper. For fully half a minute he did not move. Then he rose slowly to his feet. His eyes were green balls of flame, and out of his throat came a low and sullen snarl.

Firefly heard it. Tresor heard it. And suddenly
Firefly's tail dropped between her legs, and she ran
out midway between them and stood there, for in that
sound was death.

A step at a time Swift Lightning advanced. And as
he advanced so did Tresor, so that within thirty seconds there was hardly more than a leap between them.
In that ground stood Firefly, trembling and terrified.
And then again the swift wit of her sex possessed her.
She flung off her terror. She tossed her head play-
fully. She wagged her bushy tail in the moonlight,
and all at once she flattened herself out on her forepaws squarely between them, and the attention of
Tresor and Swift Lightning went to her. Then suddenly she ran to Swift Lightning, nipping at him play-
fully—and quick as a flash was back between them on
her forepaws again.

To Swift Lightning it was amazing and inexplicable.
He looked again at Tresor. The giant mastiff was
even larger than he. His chest was deep; his head
was massive, and his jaws were like a lion's. But it
was not the gleam of battle that shone in his eyes. It
was more a vast, wondering dismay. For he was not
a fighter. He was a woman's dog. A one-man dog.
And he worshiped a little child.

Swift Lightning, ready for the death-leap, saw what
he had never seen before. A long time ago Mistik,
the big gray wolf, had come to him like that—and

had refused to fight. But there had been no mate between them or they would have fought to the death.
His blood raced red and hot. The snarl still rumbled
in his throat, but he was beginning to understand.
The interloper was not a wolf. Neither was he a dog
as he had known dogs along the edge of the arctic sea.
*For the scent of Tresor was also the scent of Firefly,
his mate!*

His rage left him. The green fire died in his eyes.
A miracle of instinct gripped him, and he no longer
saw Firefly, but only the great mastiff. And again
there came flying back to him through the twenty dog-
generations that were gone, the ghost of Skagen, the
white man's dog. Tresor had come to greet him from
that white man's world.

For a space there in the bit of green meadow over-
looking the plains Swift Lightning, the wolf, ceased to
exist, for the Great Dane of long ago had at last
made himself heard. Foot by foot the two wondering beasts drew nearer to one another until they stood
shoulder to shoulder—and from between her forepaws Firefly's shining eyes looked up at them, filled
with a great gladness.

CHAPTER XVII

TRESOR did not remain long on the little plateau that night. He was born and bred in a different school of animal ethics from Swift Lightning, and he sensed the fact that, in this cup at the crest of the ridge, right was pitted against his might. Here had Swift Lightning preempted, and here was Swift Lightning's mate. The wolf mates for life; the dog is polygamous. But many years of life in the wilderness had given to Tresor the view-point and understanding of the wild, just as Firefly had learned those things in her few short months of companionship with Swift Lightning. Had Tresor a mate, he would have fought for her until he died. But he had no desire to fight for another's mate.

When he returned to the cabin of his master he was depressed, yet in him still lingered the great thrill of his discovery. Swift Lightning and Firefly followed him down the ridge and a short distance out into the plain; but there Swift Lightning stopped, and Firefly, seeing that he would go no farther, stopped also. She whimpered and coaxed him but when he remained fixed like a rock, looking after Tresor, she did not follow her habit of doing as she pleased in spite of him, for tonight she, too, felt subtly the existence of an unusual situation.

In Swift Lightning's brain was going on that fight to understand—and for the second time in his life he knew that he did not want to fight. With the going of Tresor he felt a loss, just as when Mistik, the big timber-wolf, had left him after weeks of comradeship on the northern barrens. Yet at the same time there was an uneasiness in his blood, a thing that disturbed him, a fear remaining from the days when the lure of men and of a ship frozen in the ice had robbed him of Firefly. It was not a fear of the flesh-and-blood rivalry of Tresor, for with him he could settle in battle as he had settled with the bear-hunting dogs of the ship. But there was one rival which he could not fight with fang —the smell of a white man's cabin, a man's hands, a woman's and a child's. And these were a part of Tresor.

During the rest of that night his efforts to draw Firefly away from the ridge and the trail of Tresor were only partly successful, for she had maneuvered their wanderings so cleverly that with dawn they were less than a mile distant. Swift Lightning was not slow to sense the change that had come over his mate. She wanted to go back. At times she would stop and stand for many minutes with her eyes on the trail behind them.

Always, after a night of wakefulness, the mates

would find a warm spot that caught the morning sun, and sleep. It was the wolf-habit, and Firefly had learned it quickly from Swift Lightning. This morning they lay down beside a big rock, and almost instantly Firefly curled herself up and buried her nose in her bushy tail. But it was with no intention of sleeping. Her clever brain was alive with excitement. Her closed eyes had the desire to shoot wide open. But she lay still, and after a little Swift Lightning thought that she was asleep. He felt better. He drew a deep breath and flattened his own big head between his forepaws. The sun fell upon him with a comfortable warmth, and he slept soundly.

Two hours later he awoke. He turned his head quickly to where Firefly should have been. She was gone. He looked about him for a few moments, expecting to see or hear her. Then he went to her bed and smelled of it. His head shot up and into his eyes came suddenly a questing anxiety, for Firefly's bed was cold, and the scent in it was faint. She had not been there for a long time.

Swift Lightning whined, and his teeth clicked in a curious way. He found her trail and began to follow it. It was no longer wandering and circuitous but led straight as a die back to the little cup of meadow in the crest of the ridge.

A great fear possessed him as he came to the tiny plateau—a fear mingled with the hope that he would find his mate there. But the meadow was empty. It was then that he made the thrilling discovery that Tresor had been there only a short time before. The scent of his big feet was warm, Firefly's trail was warm—and Swift Lightning's body grew as rigid as iron and a sullen snarl came in his throat. He trailed them slowly, a few feet at a time, watchful and alert and prepared for the vengeance of his kind. They had followed the curve of the ridge and entered a small swamp. Beyond this swamp was rising ground, and here Firefly had hesitated many minutes before going farther with Tresor. Quite frequently after this she had paused as if undecided, but always Tresor had won her on.

There was no doubt in Swift Lightning's mind now. Tresor was stealing his mate! The fire of vengeance in his blood flamed hotter and hotter, but with the curious characteristic of animal analysis he felt no bitterness toward Firefly. That his mate had betrayed him and had deserted him for another did not impress itself upon his brute consciousness as a crime for which she was accountable. Tresor was the criminal, it was Tresor he was prepared to fight, and kill if he could. That Firefly had left him in his sleep to return deliberately to the big mastiff was not even accepted as circumstantial evidence of fault in Swift Lightning's brain; but the fact that she was with Tresor at the present moment was sufficient evidence to Swift Lightning that it was with Tresor, and not Firefly, that he must deal.

And then came the thing that sent his world and his plans all to smash again. The wind was against him, and he came to an open without having sensed what was there. It was a green, meadow-like strip of plain rolling down to the river, and in the far edge of that meadow Gaston Rouget had built his new cabin. Swift Lightning was well into the open before he came upon the little rise of ground revealing to him the thrilling scene three or four hundred yards away.

Half-way between him and the cabin was Firefly, while a little beyond her stood Tresor; and outside the cabin door, watching the curious drama enacting itself before their eyes, were Gaston, Jeanne, and the baby Jeanne.

Again the rage went out of Swift Lightning, and a sudden trembling shot through his body. In his eyes grew swiftly the old gleam of understanding, of fear, and of helplessness. Where the cabin stood he saw once more the ship far north, the gray cairn of stones, the all-powerful presence of man that had lured Firefly from him before. And Tresor was a part of that presence. A second time his hatred died away, replaced by a dread that submerged all other things. He heard the woman's voice then, calling, and at the sound of that voice a new thrill shot through him. It was the voice of the woman of the log-drift Kwahoo!

His heart stood still. *Firefly was going toward her!* He gulped, swallowing the thing that rose in his throat. She had reached Tresor, and he was leading her on, and the woman was advancing a little with both arms outstretched, calling so softly that Swift Lightning could just hear her. Firefly stopped again, but Tresor went ahead of her, urging her to follow him.

A strange thing happened then. The baby Jeanne broke away from the man and ran past her mother to Tresor. Firefly did not run away but stood devouring the child with her eyes as she fondled the huge mastiff. It was then that the man began to follow the woman, also reaching out his hands and calling softly. This time Swift Lightning's fear gathered in his throat. He had not forgotten how Gaston Rouget, in the days of starvation on the great drift in the flood, had tried to kill Firefly. And Firefly had not forgotten. The scar of Gaston's knife-blade lay deep in her shoulder. For another moment Swift Lightning watched. Then he raised his head and gave a howl of warning.

It was as if Firefly had been roused from a dream when she heard the voice of her mate. In a flash she had turned. In another instant she was speeding in his direction.

Gaston pointed after her in amazement and cried, "The wolf, *ma chérie!* The wolf that came to us and killed the lynx on Kwahoo—the wolf, and ze Mon-trea-al dog!"

While they stood there, staring, Tresor turned calmly and began trotting after Firefly and Swift Lightning, who were just disappearing into the timber.

In that timber all of Swift Lightning's dread and fear turned to joy. Firefly, as if realizing that she had done him a bad turn and was penitent because of it, yipped and frisked about him, and he muzzled her forgivingly. And then, again to his utter astonishment, he looked up to see Tresor standing within half a dozen feet of them.

There was nothing at all menacing in the attitude of the huge mastiff. His appearance was most friendly and even apologetic. He was slightly wagging his long, lean tail. And Swift Lightning, meeting him eye to eye, sensed again something of that old-time comradeship which had existed between him and Mistik. He approached Tresor, and smelled him from shoulder to hip; and Tresor stood calmly, showing neither fear nor caution.

In spite of his friendship for Tresor—a friendship which it was impossible for him not to feel—Swift Lightning found himself more and more under the influence of a growing depression in the days that followed. It was impossible for him to lead Firefly any great distance away from the Rouget cabin, and scarcely a day or night passed that the big mastiff did not come to wander through forest and swamp with them. In his unreasoning way Swift Lightning knew that Firefly looked for Tresor's coming. She seemed to be always watching and waiting for him, and not infrequently left him to accompany Tresor nearer to the cabin than he would ever go.

In the lives of beasts jealousy is a formidable thing. But in Swift Lightning's soul it was an undeveloped poison. Had Tresor been a wolf, the affair would have been settled in deadly battle. But Tresor was not only a part of the cabin; he was of Firefly's own blood. He was all dog, while at times Swift Lightning felt himself an alien. For at last came the day when Firefly allowed both the older Jeanne and the baby Jeanne to touch her, and Swift Lightning smelled the scent of their hands. And it put a greater fear and a greater foreboding into his heart.

Perhaps it was merely chance and not her own quick little mind that appeared to give to Firefly an understanding of the situation. To her, Jeanne and the baby and Tresor and the cabin meant *home*. There was not much difference, after all, between this soft-voiced, dark-haired woman with the big black eyes and the fairer-haired woman Firefly had worshiped in a city far south; and there was no difference between the little Jeanne and other little Jeannes she had played with in that city. And Tresor was like the dogs that had gone up and down her street.

These things Firefly could not make Swift Lightning understand. Wholeheartedly she had accepted his wilderness, but it was impossible for her to coax or drag his wolf-blood to the door of civilization. Her friendship for Tresor was a development which, quite naturally, Swift Lightning could not see as it actually existed or it would not have perplexed him. Firefly's attitude held the mastiff quietly aloof. She never yipped at his shoulders, as she did in play at Swift Lightning's. When they lay down to rest she always curled up in her old place at Swift Lightning's side. And Tresor kept his distance. Twice Firefly had plainly let him know her attitude toward him. Twice her white teeth had slashed his shoulder, and he understood clearly that she belonged to Swift Lightning.

It was a week after Firefly's first visit to the cabin that Swift Lightning ran a thorn deep into his foot. For two or three days he limped about, then found himself a cool, deep-shadowed spot near a pool of water and gave himself up to a torment of sickness. The foot swelled until it was twice its normal size, and a fever developed in his blood. The first day of his sickness Firefly remained near him, licking his paw and watching him with her bright eyes. Tresor came and for a time lay in the shade with them. When he went home Firefly showed no desire to accompany him. The second day she went with him, and returned in half an hour. But that night, when she hunted under the moon, it was Tresor who hunted with her.

It was the fourth day of his sickness that Swift Lightning awoke from a sleep early in the afternoon to find Firefly gone. He dragged himself to his feet, whining for her, and limped to the pool. He lapped up the water with his hot tongue and stood for a minute or two, listening. He lay down again, and in his throat was a whimpering note of loneliness and of grief. And yet even then he felt no desire for vengeance upon Tresor. An hour passed, and suddenly he drew his head alert at the sound of padded footfalls. Another moment, and Tresor stood before him.

In the eyes of the two big beasts was the same question. Where was Firefly? Swift Lightning looked beyond Tresor. Tresor sniffed the air and waited expectantly for sight or sound of her. Perhaps not more than a minute passed before understanding flashed between them. Firefly had not been with Tresor. And she was not with Swift Lightning. To Swift Lightning's questioning whine a responsive whine rose in Tresor's throat. He began to sniff in the edge of the thickets, but there were so many of Firefly's trails that his effort to pick up the last one was futile. He came back to Swift Lightning and stretched out his great body near him, and for half an hour they waited with hardly a movement.

Then Tresor rose again to his feet, and with another whine to Swift Lightning trotted slowly into the forest in the direction of the Rouget cabin.

A mile away, where an arm of the River du Rocher came down from the north, Firefly was squatted in a thicket, her eyes shining with a great excitement. Not more than fifty feet from her was the smoldering camp-fire of a Dog-Rib Indian. It was an hour ago that Meea, the Indian, had run his canoe ashore and built that fire. He had cooked a fish over it. And because the only other living creature with him had tried to steal that roasting fish he had whipped her within an inch of her life. Firefly had heard her howling, and a little later she had stolen into the thicket, and it was from there that she first saw Narcissus.

A white man was responsible for that name, and the Dog-Rib had changed it to a guttural "Waps." Waps, if not the homeliest, was at least the second most un-beautiful dog in the world, wherefore her master had loved her and called her Narcissus. She was an Aire-dale and not much more than half as large as Firefly. Her hair was a faded rust-color and wiry. She was thin and angular, and her head was a couple of sizes too big for her body—for although better than two years old, she had never outgrown the physical handi-caps of her puppyhood. Her whiskers, sticking out straight in front of her face, were longer and almost as stiff as porcupine quills, and through this brush her bright little eyes watched with caution the sleeping Indian and also her surroundings. A year ago someone had stolen her from her master, and recently she had fallen into Meea's hands. And Meea hated her. He had given her a more than usually hard beating today. Then he ate his fish and rolled over for a nap.

For many minutes after the Dog-Rib had begun his siesta Firefly did not move. Something that thrilled her was at work in her brain. Two and two were trying to add themselves into four, and all the time the wind that brought her the scent of the camp stirred her with still greater desire to attract the attention of the stranger dog. And suddenly Waps saw Firefly standing out in the open, wagging her tail in a way that no other real dog in the world could fail to understand. Two minutes later they were smelling noses, and the Airedale's knotty tail was beating the air excitedly.

It was not difficult for Firefly to make herself understood. "I've got something to show you," she seemed to say. "Come with me." And Waps, beaten until her ribs were sore, followed without hesitation.

It was an hour later that Jeanne Rouget, looking from the door of her cabin, saw a thing that made her call softly to Gaston, who was making new snowshoes for the coming of winter. Gaston went to the door and looked over her shoulder, and Jeanne heard plainly the amazement that seemed to catch in a lump in his throat. For close to the cabin were three dogs, and not one of them was Swift Lightning.

Gaston, with his eyes on Waps, whispered as if to himself, *"Tonnere!* It ees ze Montrea-al dog with ze wire in hees face! I have never seen dog lak that up here. I tell you——"

"Sh-h," whispered Jeanne.

Tresor was smelling of Waps, and every wiry hair in the little Airedale's body seemed atremble with the joy of his attention. Then Gaston saw Tresor's tail wagging like a club, and all at once his great hulk began hopping about Waps as if he had gone mad.

Firefly, realizing that her mission was done, turned suddenly and began trotting away toward the forest— and Swift Lightning. This time Tresor did not notice her going. Proud as a monarch, he was leading Waps to the open door of the cabin where stood Jeanne and Gaston, wondering at the simple miracle of life which had unfolded itself under their eyes.

Tresor, at last, had found a mate.

CHAPTER XVIII

THE glorious spring of the Northland, with its bursting life and happy song, had come and gone. Summer was ending. Red autumn was near.

Marvelously had these two seasons passed over the vast and unmapped regions of wilderness between the Great Slave and the River du Rocher, a thousand miles north of civilization. After deep snows of winter a spring had come such as the few forest people there had never seen before. And summer had given fruitage to its promise.

For three months the land had overflowed with the milk and honey of a smiling God. In those months bushes hung heavy with fruit that was rich and sweet. In the soft grass, in deep swamps, even in the trees hung treasure for the gathering. Underfoot were wild strawberries so thick and red that the crush of them smeared the boots of Gaston Rouget and Jeanne when they went out to gather them. Black currants, big as the end of a finger, hung in festoons of shining jet on the mother-bushes; raspberries and saskatoons covered the ground where they grew; and the ash trees, with their clusters of berries, delicious in preserves and coveted by all things wild, were so heavy with fruit that in the sun half a mile away a tree looked like a red blaze, its branches breaking with the weight of their burden.

It seemed, this season, that Nature had grown wanton and intemperate, and that she must rob other years to pay for this; for she had not only given good measure, but it was pressed down and running over. And the wilderness world seemed to sing with its contentment and its happiness. The few people who lived in it here and there were laying in their stores for another winter. And the wild things were living in the extravagance of a superabundant present. The little bears, this summer, were as wide as they were long, so fat were they. All things, hoof and claw and wing, multiplied in a land of plenty.

Now autumn with its first cool night breaths was not far away, and with its approach came a new thrill into the blood of all living things. It was like a tonic, coming to rouse them after a long period of idleness and overfeeding. The forests, faintly at first, began to reveal the delicate artistry that very soon would blazen more loudly and with resplendent triumph the presence of September—"the Moon in which the deer rub their horns." For even now, with August not entirely gone, patches of gold and yellow began to appear in bolder tints with each passing day amid the green and purple masses of forest and swamp.

One night, as they sat under the stars in front of

their cabin of logs, Gaston Rouget and his dark-haired Jeanne heard the honk of geese high up over their heads; and Gaston's fingers picked at the strings of his old violin, as he hummed words that had come strangely into the far north from the country of Temiskaming and Timagami. And Jeanne, dreaming of that land where she was born, joined with him still more softly:

"Oh! the fur fleets sing on Temiskaming
   As the ashen paddles bend,
And the crews carouse at Rupert's house,
   At the sullen winter's end.

But my days are done where the lean wolves run,
   And I ripple no more the path
Where the gray geese race 'cross the red moon's face
   From the white wind's arctic wrath."

And then suddenly, as if in answer, a long and lonely howl came from far away in the forest that reached southward. Gaston's hand sought Jeanne's, and with a bit of awe in his voice he said, "It is the wolf-dog, my Jeanne. The summer is almost over now, and very soon he will leave us entirely and go back forever to the wild. When the wolf packs begin to run—then he will go. And—*tonnere*, I am sorry!"

Two miles away Swift Lightning howled. Only once did he turn his muzzle up to the stars and give voice to his loneliness. Then, alone, he sat at the edge of a yellow bit of plain, and watched and listened, gripped by the thing that was growing heavier upon him as the days of summer came to a close.

It was not that he yearned for the land of the wolf packs or the grim tundras and empty plains of the arctic coast. Months of plentitude in the southern forests had made him forget many of the things that had happened there. Memory no longer recalled to him the days and weeks and months of starvation and fighting for life. In those ways is Nature kind to the beast. She does not destroy his memories of what has gone; but softly she puts them to sleep, and dormant they lie until something comes to rouse them to life again—perhaps years afterward.

And now to Swift Lightning had come the thing that was eating like a sickness inside him. Firefly, a white man's dog, a woman's dog, a dog from the land of little white children, had come to love more and more the cabin of Gaston Rouget. At that cabin were Tresor and Waps; there also were laughter and song. Because of these things Firefly rejoiced, for she knew what it meant to have a woman's gentle hand stroke her head again, and she lived once more in the laughter and tears of a child's grief and play.

Swift Lightning, with the wolf-blood in his veins making its last great fight to win him back to savagery, did not understand.

It was man. That was the poison. Man the destroyer. Man the all-powerful and the all-feared.

Man the lure. For nature, in placing that riotous and steadily growing drop of dog in Swift Lightning, had set him between the devil and the deep sea. Nothing that had ever happened between man and himself had he forgotten. While the wolf in his blood made him dread the man-god and fear him, the spirit of Skagen filled him with the yearning for his comradeship.

It was that yearning that had taken him to the white man's cabin on the edge of the glacier-slash, where O'Connor had fired at him with a rifle. It was this same yearning that had more than once lured him close to man, and always man had met him as an enemy. It was man that had put the hot fire of a bullet into his shoulder, man who had slashed him with a seal spear, man who had set the horde of ship's dogs on him.

For many weeks Firefly had worked bravely to bring him to the cabin of Gaston Rouget. But she had never lured him farther than the edge of the clearing in which the cabin stood. More than once the man and the woman had watched, wondering if the miracle would happen and if Swift Lightning would come to them. For in their hearts, because of the wonder of Firefly's matehood, was a love for this great gray beast of the forests.

Night after night and day after day Firefly went to him with Tresor and Waps; and together the four wandered in the forests or ran under the stars. But always at the end the three went back to the cabin, and Swift Lightning remained alone. In these hours of his aloneness, as the autumn came, the thing inside him ate more viciously at his vitals. In a last mighty surge the wolf that was in him rose in fierce demand, and he listened to the wolf-howl as he had not listened before. As the nights grew cooler and the days grew shorter, as the loon cried more shrilly, and the moose began to give their challenges, and the wolf packs to gather, he stood uncertain of himself—almost ready to yield up all that he had won.

Tonight he stood in the edge of the little plain, and sent out that single howl. Firefly, already on her way to join him, stood still in the deep forest and listened to it; and in the wild note of it was something that drew a whimpering whine from her and stirred within her a new kind of fear, another understanding.

She was alone when she came to him. She had stolen away from Tresor and his little Airedale mate; and Swift Lightning, when he made sure they were not behind her, muzzled her neck and whined his gladness. Then, with his muzzle in her silken coat, his nostrils tasted again the poison that had robbed him of the glorious days before the big flood and the discovery of Gaston Rouget's cabin. For that day the woman had fondled Firefly, and the child had played with her, and Gaston, smoking his strong black pipe, had picked swamp-burs out of her hair after supper.

The poison hung like a deadly incense about her. To Swift Lightning this man-smell had become the evil of all evils. It was his curse. Not a dog, and yet not a wolf, it had both attracted and repelled him. Many times he had answered its call, and always it had hurt him, or tried to hurt him. And now it was robbing him of his mate.

In his throat grew a low snarl as he smelled of Firefly's yellow body. It was not that he felt anger toward her. She knew that, and flattened herself on her belly and watched him anxiously from between her forepaws. For just as Swift Lightning knew that the cabin had made a great change in his mate, so did Firefly sense the impending change in Swift Lightning.

For many weeks he had not gone far away. He could always be found when she wanted him and he had fought constantly the wolf in him that he might be near her. But now a redder light was growing in his eyes, and he was looking afar. Firefly did not reason that it was the cabin and the rivalry of a man and a woman and a child that were driving him back into the savagery of twenty generations of wolf forebears. But the fact that she was losing this mate, who had fought and triumphed and lived for her, became a growing thing within her.

Tonight she was different. For a week she had not played and scampered round Swift Lightning. Yet each night or day she had returned to the cabin and

had tried to lure him back. Now, as she watched him
looking off into the star-mist, there came to her from
the distance a wolf-howl, and she saw Swift Lightning's body grow tense. The rivalry of that distant
call struck to her soul, and she wriggled to his feet;
Swift Lightning relaxed and muzzled her for an instant in the old joyous way, forgetful of the poison of
man and cabin.

It was he and not Firefly that led the way tonight.
And it was *away* from the cabin. Always, at the far
edge of this strip of plain, she had stopped. Farther
from the cabin she would not go. But now, when Swift
Lightning struck into the country beyond, she followed him. Strangely he sensed the fact that she was
not the old Firefly. There was a mystery about her,
a mystery that held him, that made him travel slowly,
that made him stop when she stopped. And when he
saw that she was following him where she had refused
to follow before, his splendid head went up as in the
days of old, when he alone possessed her. And when
the wolf-howl came many times in the hours that followed he paid no heed to it. Frequently Firefly paused
to rest, and at the end of the second hour she lay down
in the edge of a giant windfall of trees, and Swift
Lightning made no further effort to urge her on.

All the rest of that night she did not move. And
the next day she went no farther than the edge of a
tiny creek a few yards away, and still farther back in

the shelter of the windfall she found herself a place
to lie in. Swift Lightning was puzzled. He was uneasy. The great mystery thrilled him, and yet he did
not fully understand. But the glory of the old days
had returned to him.

Again he possessed Firefly—alone. The second
night she made no effort to return to the cabin, and
this night the wolf-howl might have been a hundred
miles away for all the attention Swift Lightning paid
to it. Alone he hunted. He brought in two rabbits
and laid them at Firefly's feet.

In the gray dawn of the third day he returned again
from his hunt in the near bush. He was not gone
long. But a great change had come under the windfall. And as he went in, his eyes glowing, his body
trembling with the thrill of the new thing that came to
him, mystery fell away and a great understanding
surged upon him. From the gray-dawn gloom of her
nest Firefly's eyes glowed at him softly, and there was
a joyous, whimpering note in her golden throat—and
in the presence of that miracle under the windfall he
stood for many minutes like a beast carven out of
wood.

For Firefly had come into the glory of motherhood.
And the children she bore were Swift Lightning's
children.

CHAPTER XIX

ONLY the softly whispering winds in the tree tops sing the songs of motherhood among beasts in the deep forests; only the low-rippling joy of running water joins in its exultation, only the unseen choruses of the earth breathe its glorification. And this dawn, when Swift Lightning's children were born, the world about the windfall seemed to know. A little woodthrush just outside the door sang of new life until its throat seemed like to burst. Over Firefly's head, questing its breakfast in an overhanging tree a red squirrel paused to chatter its greeting to the breaking day; and in the east the sun threw up its banners of red and gold, and all the world, it seemed, rejoiced.

Under the windfall Firefly's heart was beating a new and wonderful pæan. It was her first motherhood, and every fiber of her was attuned to the glorious thrill of it. And outside—in the soul of the great gray beast who had come into the heritage of his first family—the answer to that thrill was like the vibrating tremor of strange music. For a space it dazed him. And then he was uneasy. Again and again in the first hour after his marvelous discovery he trotted back and forth in front of the windfall. Five times in that hour he went in close to Firefly and smelled of the tiny, whimpering life which he could not see; and each time when he went forth again his head was higher and his step quicker, and in his eyes a deeper fire. For at last had he come face to face with fatherhood.

That fatherhood meant more to him than it would have meant to a dog, for nature had made the law that a wolf should have but one mate, year in and year out; and to Swift Lightning, monogamous in his mate-hood, the little creatures under the windfall were flesh of his flesh and blood of his blood, and for them he was ready to give up his life if the call came to that, just as he was ready to fight and die for the mother who had given them birth. Therein, in a moral way, was Swift Lightning the wolf greater than the dog.

It came very soon upon him that this windfall into which Firefly had crept was the one sacred place in all the world, a place which must not be desecrated, a place to be defended. It was that first instinct of savagery that possessed him the sixth time he came out from the wonderful nest under the tumbled tree tops and logs. He went completely round the windfall, not questingly and inquiringly, but openly and defiantly. It had become suddenly *his* property, no matter who or what had inhabited it before, and he was almost eager that something should challenge his sovereignty that he might prove to all living things the absolutism of his empire.

Since that first golden night when he had mated with Firefly long ago, he had not felt quite so ridiculously eager to do something; and at last his energy found a vent in scouring the near-by bush for game. Before the day was fairly under way he had brought three big rabbits to his mate. This, again, was the wolf in him, and Firefly, though she did not eat, twice thrust out her red tongue to his face in grateful appreciation. Bred in the ways of the dog it was not beyond her to comprehend the devotion and the chivalry of the wolf. And she did not snap and snarl at him as a mother dog usually does at another dog's intrusion. Each time Swift Lightning came into the windfall she welcomed him with her glowing eyes, her body trembled with pleasure, and in her throat was always a greeting note of gladness.

And each time Swift Lightning tried harder and harder *to see what was there!*

He knew; he had heard the faint little voices; and yet—because of the gloom and Firefly's protecting body—he had not seen. At last he dared to seek gently, and when the cool tip of his nose touched for the first time one of the soft little bits of life snuggling in the warmth of Firefly's hair he jumped back almost as if he had touched the hot end of an iron. In another irresistible fit of zeal he went out and hunted until he killed a fourth rabbit, which he added to the untouched offering in the nest.

Not until late that afternoon did Firefly come out from under the windfall, and then it was only to go to the little creek and drink. She came out again at dusk. All that night Swift Lightning did not go away from the windfall. The next morning he began hunting again. The rabbits were so plentiful that it was not difficult for him to kill, and Firefly ate one of the fresh rabbits that day. Once more his cup of happiness was full to the brim and running over, and inasmuch as his mate could not play or run with him his energy continued to find its chief vent in hunting. Rabbits piled up about Firefly until her bright eyes peered over a barricade of them when Swift Lightning entered the windfall.

A little later came the inevitable. An unwholesome odor began to fasten itself upon the home. It grew steadily stronger until, on the fifth day after the first kill, Swift Lightning came home with another rabbit to find his mate slyly busy in a process of house-cleaning. One after another Firefly brought out nine rabbits, and each rabbit she covered with leaves and mold at a distance of twenty or thirty yards from the windfall.

One day, not so very long after this, Firefly had another home-coming surprise in store for her mate when he returned from the hunt. For out into a pool of warm sunlight she had brought her babies, and there Swift Lightning saw them clearly for the first time, tumbling about the golden body of their mother, a marvelous sight for the eyes of fatherhood. It must be that his heart swelled with new pride and new joy, and surely Firefly's heart was singing within her, for Nature had shown no disappointing favoritism in that family of theirs. There were two little Fireflies, tawny and yellow, and two little Swift Lightnings, silver and gray.

In the splendid days and nights that followed, Firefly had not much time to think of Gaston Rouget's cabin and her friends there, for her children were lively little creatures and their demands were insistent and tireless. In fact the failing of overindulgence that sometimes comes with first motherhood held her firmly in its grip. The proudest moment in her life was when this brood waddled after her to the little creek one day, and the proudest moment in Swift Lightning's was when this same little brood acted like young cannibals every time he brought a rabbit in. They did not eat the flesh but they had a lot of fun pulling hair and fur. During these same days, in the cabin of Gaston Rouget Firefly and Swift Lightning were given up for all time.

But in Firefly, in spite of her happiness, the lure of "home" was only asleep and not dead. After a time it began to waken slowly, and inside her the desire grew more and more to take her little family to the cabin in the clearing. For the nights were chilly now.

And instinct urged her to find a warmer home for her puppies than the old windfall.

What would have happened soon after that, it is difficult to say. Many things might have happened. As it was Fate drove straight home with one of the most dramatic episodes in Swift Lightning's life. To achieve her end she sent *Yootin Wetikoo.*

Yootin Wetikoo was neither red nor white, nor was it of flesh and blood. It was, in short, what the Indians call the "devil-wind." This "devil-wind" did not come frequently. But when it did come it was believed that all the devils in the land had gone mad in their desire to disrupt the world. To white men it was neither a thing of mystery nor of bad spirits. It was the northwest tornado.

This year, even though the month was late September, it was preceded by a veritable inferno of thunder and lightning. Half an hour of that and the cataclysm broke over the windfall. For a space the sky was a sea of electrical fire, and the earth trembled with a shock of the mighty atmospheric convulsions far up above the forests. Firefly cowered back in her nest, and her puppies snuggled themselves close, whimpering against her body. Swift Lightning, as if to protect his possessions from the wrath of the storm, lay close to the opening of the windfall, his eyes staring into the night and reflecting the lightning's flare.

For not more than a quarter of an hour there was a

deluge of rain, and then thunder and lightning and rain raced into the east and steadily died away. After that followed a silence, terrible and black. In that silence Swift Lightning could hear distinctly the sound of the suddenly flooded little rivulet and the dripping of water from the boughs of the trees. And then, from far away, there came faintly a low moaning.

There was no break in that dismal and foreboding sound. It grew slowly and steadily nearer until it was like the sound of a waterfall. Swift Lightning could not see, but what he heard was something that had never come to his ears in the fiercest storms that had ever swept over the pole. The path of the tornado was not more than half a mile wide, but five miles away Gaston Rouget and Jeanne were listening to the roar of it. In that path was a snapping and rending of trees. Tall spruce and cedars were torn up by the roots as if they were weeds. Trails were choked. Open spaces were suddenly filled with the débris of ruin and desolation. Now and then, out of the heart of the wind, a giant hand seemed to drive straight down— and when this happened anything that was in the path of that hand was swept aside as if by a mighty giant broom. The roar was terrific. It was as if the world were coming to an end.

From straight over the windfall shot down one of the terrible, destroying spear-thrusts of the tornado. It veered slightly, so that the edge of it struck Swift

Lightning's side of the windfall. In that explosion of the wind he felt the crash of logs and tree tops and débris about him. The edge of the windfall was twisted and torn into pieces, and suddenly there fell upon him out of the blackness a great and crushing weight.

Only twenty feet away Firefly's nest remained almost undisturbed. In it she shivered and muzzled her puppies as the tornado roared overhead and went on. In the trail it had blasted through the forest fell another deluge of rain. Half an hour later the old silence hovered over the stricken timber-land.

In the first of that silence Firefly heard a strange sound from Swift Lightning. It was not a yelp. It was not a howl. It was not a dog's cry of distress. For Swift Lightning, when it came to bearing pain, was *wolf*—and in the agony that was upon him now it was hardly more than a throat-note that he made. But Firefly heard it. She whimpered a reply, and in answer to that whimper came a gasping, moaning sigh. Half a minute later she had made her way to him through a tangle of débris. He was no longer *in* the windfall, but in the open. And over him, crushing him into the earth, lay the butt of a tree twice as thick through as a man's body.

In Firefly's head was the brain of the collie—the brain which, at times, seems almost human—and for hours that night she dug to save the life of her mate.

She sensed the nearness of death, and she gave herself utterly to her task. After storm the skies cleared. The moon and stars came out. And still she dug. Her puppies whimpered and called. But she tore at the earth with teeth and claws until she was exhausted and her feet were raw. Even then it was impossible for her to save Swift Lightning. His body was crushed. One of his legs was broken. Slowly the life was dying out of him.

In the early dawn Firefly gave up her task. But in the last extreme one thing always rises up in the vision of the collie dog. It is man. And with her last strength Firefly covered the five miles between the windfall and the cabin of Gaston Rouget. Before the door of the cabin she barked and scratched until both Gaston and Jeanne rolled out of their bed to see what the tumult meant. What they saw drew a strange cry from each. For Firefly's paws left stains of blood on the cabin floor. She was panting and almost ready to drop. But she ran back half-way to the edge of the forest—once—twice—three times—barking for Gaston Rouget to follow her. And, at last, understanding that something of mystery lay out there beyond the edge of the clearing, he put on his clothes, caught up his rifle, and followed.

The sun was well up, and the last of life was fading slowly from Swift Lightning's eyes when a strange vision stood for a moment before him. It was man. And Firefly was with him. And then he could no longer see. But he heard sounds, indistinctly for a time, and after that all was blackness. Gaston Rouget, with a broken sapling for a lever, labored with the will of a giant at the great log—and two hours later he returned to the cabin in the clearing with a strange burden in his arms.

Swift Lightning knew that things were happening. His eyes opened, and he saw the wonder of it all. But he was helpless. He could not move. Gaston was holding his foreleg straight out on a narrow slab of flat wood, Jeanne was binding it round and round with long strips of cloth—and he had no strength to snap at them. They were talking to him, and when it was done the woman's hand stroked his head. Just beyond them was the little Jeanne, big-eyed and staring, and at the door, held back by Gaston's command, were Tresor and Waps. Then he was put on a soft blanket in a corner of the cabin and the man went out, taking Tresor and Waps with him. For a long time he lay there. Frequently the woman came to him and put her hand on him, unafraid, and placed water and fresh meat under his nose. And after that—a long time afterward—the man returned, and with him this time was Firefly, jumping up excitedly about a big basket which he carried. This basket Gaston opened, and from it, one by one, he drew out Swift Lightning's two little sons and two little daughters and put them down on the blanket beside him. And Swift Lightning, overwhelmed by the miracle of it, closed his eyes and sighed.

That sigh was the sigh of Skagen, the Great Dane. Never after this would Swift Lightning fear the touch of the white man's hand, for the beginning of his dream had come true. And Gaston, answering the question of Jeanne's lips, shrugged his shoulders and laughed softly.

"Yes, he will live, *ma chérie*. It will be many weeks before he runs again, and he will run always with a limp—but he will live. And when that time comes he will not go very far away. *Non*. There is dog in his eyes. And he will love you. Not me, Gaston Rouget, big and black and hairy, but you, my Jeanne. *Oui*— he will love you—*par dessus la tête!*—or I miss my guess. See—he is looking at you now! Is it not so? Do you not see the dog shining there? I think he has come home—after a long time. And I tell you that he will never again go very far away."

THE END

www.ingramcontent.com/pod-product-compliance
Lightning Source LLC
Chambersburg PA
CBHW011522240626
47154CB00009B/2926